Stigma & The Cave

Also by D. H. Melhem

POETRY

Notes on 94th Street

Rest in Love

Children of the House Afire/More Notes on 94th Street

Country: An Organic Poem

Poems for You (chapbook)

Conversation with a Stonemason

New York Poems

PROSE

Blight: A Novel

Heroism in the New Black Poetry: Introductions and Interviews

Gwendolyn Brooks: Poetry and the Heroic Voice

Reaching Exercises: The IWWG Workshop Book

EDITOR

Mosaic: Poems from an IWWG Workshop

A Different Path: An Anthology of RAWI (co-editor, Leila Diab)

MUSICAL DRAMA

Children of the House Afire

Stigma & The Cave

TWO NOVELS

D. H. Melhem

For Patrick Connolly
With warmest esteem and appreciation
DHMelhem
8.8.08

SYRACUSE UNIVERSITY PRESS

Syracuse University Press, Syracuse, New York 13244–5160

First Edition 2007
07 08 09 10 11 12   6 5 4 3 2 1

Stigma and *The Cave* are the second and third books of a trilogy titled *Patrimonies.*
The first book of the trilogy, *Blight*, was published in 1995 by Riverrun Press, Inc.,
New York, and is distributed by Syracuse University Press.

The excerpt of poetry on page 113 is reprinted from "Mrs. Pink Plastic," appearing in *New York
Poems.* Copyright © 2005 by D. H. Melhem and published by Syracuse University Press.

My profound gratitude goes to Mary Selden Evans for her continuing faith in my work. I am
indebted once more to a superb publishing team at Syracuse University Press. Fred Wellner
provided artwork for a stunning cover. Richard Derus and Rainelle Burton carefully reviewed an
earlier version of *Stigma*. I thank Gregory M. Vogel, first reader of my prose. Gregory, Dana Vogel,
and George Meyer sustain me in all ways.

The paper used in this publication meets the minimum requirements of
American National Standard for Information Sciences—Permanence of
paper for Printed Library Materials, ANSI Z39.48–1984.∞ ™

For a listing of books published and distributed by Syracuse University Press,
visit our Web site at SyracuseUniversityPress.syr.edu.

ISBN-13: 978-0-8156-0882-0   ISBN-10: 0-8156-0882-9

Library of Congress Cataloging-in-Publication Data
Melhem, D. H.
Stigma; and, The cave : two novels / D.H. Melhem.—1st ed.
p. cm.
"Stigma and The cave are the second and third books of a trilogy titled Patrimonies.
The first book of the trilogy, Blight"—T.p. verso.
ISBN-13: 978–0–8156–0882–0 (pbk. : alk. paper)
ISBN-10: 0–8156–0882–9 (pbk. : alk. paper)
1. Political fiction, American. I. Melhem, D. H. Cave. II. Title. III. Title: Cave.
PS3563.E442S75 2007
813'.54—dc22   2006037894

Manufactured in the United States of America

For my beloved family

for the shades of my parents

for Claudia, who saw it whole

for my companions in peace

and with homage to those

who wrote in harsh times

yet had their say

D. H. Melhem's numerous awards for poetry and prose include an American Book Award, a National Endowment for the Humanities fellowship, and three Pushcart Prize nominations. Her poetry collections *Notes on 94th Street* and *Children of the House Afire* have been recently republished by Syracuse University Press in an expanded edition titled *New York Poems*. *Blight*, the first novel in the trilogy *Patrimonies*, is also distributed by Syracuse University Press and is in development as a feature film. Melhem serves as vice-president of the International Women's Writing Guild.

Contents

STIGMA

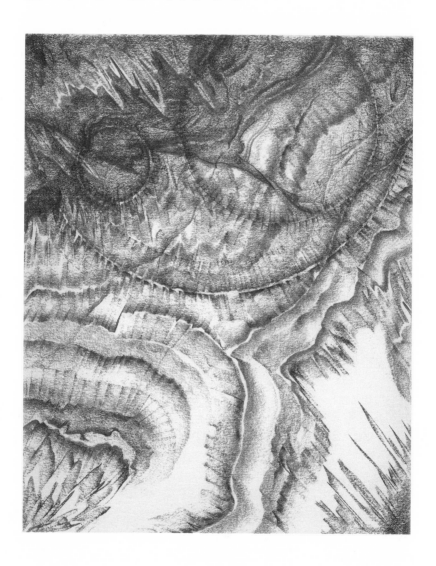

J.

I focus on the figure of my father, in whose wisdom my universe revolved. The long past turns my cell away from its window to his window, where he sits in a comfortable armchair, with his back to the glass. Memory whirls me past the Yard that dangles the body of a young man—about my son Michael's age?—like a gray chicken, head askew, listening. Bare chicken feet like those in a butcher shop.

Serafina sends me to the butcher who holds a fowl at my nose.

"You want the feet?" Its feet bright yellow, distinct from the plucked flesh so freshly seized from running. "You want the feet?" he asks. "No."

"Feet make a stronger soup," my wife rebukes softly. The whole chicken must be taken. The whole man.

Serafina! Are you nearby? Are you alive?

The cell is the length of my cot and two feet wider. A corner beneath the window holds a square of sand to receive my wastes. Not much shit on this diet—porridge, coffee, garbage soup. It stinks here. Of disinfectant. Of me.

Once a week we get a pail and shovel to replace the sand. You could say I live in a gray cement toilet. Wear a gray paper smock—we call them "mocks"—with a large red circle like a target over my heart. I am barefoot. I have chicken feet.

Memories huddle like fugitives. My father, tall. His stony scowl separates two worlds: family, a kind of mind; strangers, matter to be observed. At a distance. (We could catch diseases or learn bad ways or waste time or get into trouble that lay in ambush everywhere.) My rebellious older brother fled into early marriage and left our town. He was killed a year later in one of the ever more common military actions. I'm young. I was not close to him. My father hides his grief. My mother never seemed well after that. I remember her as a fading fragrance in the room.

My father's house. Later becoming my house. Small evergreen bushes in front. The fence, broken by a gang of kids. Mended. Broken again. Cedar shingles turning black. Antimacassars covering worn spots on my father's chair and on the sofa. My sons — Michael chasing Charles into the back yard. Serafina making dinner. I close my eyes and the kitchen appears, smelling of holiday turkey, drippings crackling in a pan. I can taste the house.

A Guard sprays disinfectant. I cough. He shoots an extra dose at me. "Wanna smell good in case you go to the Love Room!" He laughs and moves on. I want to kill him.

"You need a wife," says my father. He means, "We need a wife." He is lonely after my mother's death. He doesn't know that I've fallen in love with a young woman who makes regular deposits at my bank and seems to wait for my window. We exchange a few words each time. I say the name on her check: "Serafina." She smiles. A beautiful name, I tell her. It suits her gentle personality. She has just lost her own mother to cancer.

We go out to the movies or to a simple restaurant, share our grief. It lessens when we are together. She works as a clerk in a state lottery office. We talk of marriage and having children.

The first time I bring her home she cooks a nice dinner, a rich stew. My father seems to relish it and the good apple pie and strong coffee. "You cook well," he says, as if sealing a bargain. Serafina and I are married in a civil ceremony and we take a little trip to Niagara Falls. "It isn't safe anywhere!" my father warns. My bride moves in. We speak of getting our own place but my father needs us and besides, everyone seems to be getting poorer. There is inflation, banks close branches and merge (we are anxious about my job, not Serafina's). My father is still a supervisor at a chemical plant. One evening a week he disappears. I suspect, even hope that he has a woman. A few years later he retires and the disappearances cease. He develops a persistent cough. I blame the chemicals at his plant. Loyal to his employer who provides a small pension even after the labor union has been crushed, he discourages my thoughts.

Serafina becomes pregnant, works for a few months, then gives up her job. She looks like an angel. Her skin, which always had a pinkish glow, seems translucent. Her eyes appear larger, as if they see more of the world. She wears a little smile that makes me want to kiss her when my father is not there. We take picnic lunches to the park and sit by the green pond (never late, because there are more incidents with youngsters and muggings in our once-tranquil suburb).

"You're taking chances!" my father warns.

Giving birth changes Serafina. She's proud of her body. Something has firmed in her. Though her dark hair is still luxurious and invites caresses, she keeps some of her pregnancy weight. Her spirit seems to bulk up her figure, or does her figure bulk her spirit? Traces of spunkiness irritate my father. Serafina privately calls herself "the help." She deserves an occasional day off.

Michael's birth disrupts our lives. "Your wife"—she becomes nameless when my father is displeased—"has come home too soon from the hospital," he complains. "In the old days a woman stayed for a week."

"I'm not sick," she tells him. "Our insurance won't cover more time." Soon he again insists on a fixed dinnertime, his closest approach to religious faith. "Michael," she counters, "must be fed."

"Give him a bottle!" my father growls at the stairs.

"I'm trying to nurse him!" she shouts from our room.

"I'll serve us," I say. "Dinner's ready. It's in the pot."

"It's always in the pot!" he shouts at me.

No wonder we have a colicky baby. So much crying. In a few weeks Serafina gives up trying to nurse Michael and puts him on the bottle. Her milk dries up and she blames my father. Michael never seems to stop crying. He won't let me hold him.

"I saw a man urinating in the street! I saw it from my window! We're supposed to have more police," my father says.

"We have more police," I tell him.

"Order begins at home. You can't just push dinnertime around," he complains as Serafina brings Michael downstairs and places him in his bassinet. "Dinnertime" sounds like a hefty person.

Michael never takes to my father who blames Serafina. The baby squirms at his touch and pushes his hand away from the carriage. Then again, Michael always squirms.

My father is different with Charles. Maybe Charles is different too. It is strange to watch the man open his arms and see my son run to him. He teaches the boy to play checkers, then chess. A good way to keep him prisoner, I think uncharitably. Michael grows rebellious like my late brother.

The boys go to school but there is nothing for them to do afterward. No sports or clubs. The town can barely pay its teachers. Classes are large. Rowdy children are a problem. It's better for our sons to be at home more. Serafina works part-time at the lottery office. My father disapproves of television—its violence and sex and its dumb cartoons—so it's rarely on. Reception is bad anyway.

My father is dying. He lies in his brass bed, refusing to see doctors or visitors. He has no friends and loathes doctors for not having saved his wife. He calls out the name "Aunt." She is a woman with whom he and his father boarded for years after his mother ran back to the "Old Country," a mysterious, unnameable place in Britain. He tells me about Aunt's apron with its two deep pockets. "The right one—that was for handkerchiefs to cover laughter and tears. The left one—that was for candy she offered me." Then he calls out: "Abandon hope, all ye who enter here!"

"What?" I ask. He is much better educated than I am. And at free schools, too. No such colleges left. I had a certificate and was good at math. Good at something.

Finally he becomes silent. I sponge-bathe him and change his underwear. He looks at my mother's gold-framed picture on the wall and opens his mouth to sigh. He coughs dark phlegm into large white handkerchiefs. Serafina must wash them but he will not let her touch him. He refuses food and feebly waves away the doctor I insisted on calling, the doctor who returns to pronounce him dead. His face, fierce and pale, refuses that last intruder, death, a peaceable entry.

Undertakers come to carry the body to the funeral parlor and then to the crematorium. Michael and Charles bounce into the room. They shout and dance around the stretcher, and poke the body bag with grotesque delight. The men, unnerved, hastily wheel their charge out the door.

Serafina is horrified. I fear the boys may be unhinged by shock.

Charles shows me a star on his wrist and I see the same mark on Michael's. "I have a tattoo!" shouts Michael.

"Me too!" laughs Charles. I recall reading of these stars and other designs as products of a drug syndicate that preys on children. The tattoos are patches laden with LSD and other narcotics to lure children into addiction. Such criminals should be killed! There are severe penalties, usually death, yet the practice continues.

I call the doctor again. He seems unimpressed. He tells me to wash their wrists with soap and lecture our sons. Momma says to me, "We caught him smoking and drinking, and now this!" She blames Michael who seeks adventure and finds school dull. In a few hours the boys quiet down as the doctor predicted, but we are shaken.

"Order begins at home!" my father is shouting. His ominous words roar over me.

S.

I wish my hands were big as hams to cover my head. I run my fingers over the stubble. These are not my fingers they are Joseph's, stroking my dark hair, my lost hair stolen by the prison for "sanitary" reasons. When I pray I can hear Joseph teasing me with "I am an atheist and you are my little churchmouse!" It is a mild joke because my mother sent me to Sunday

School, before Church was discouraged by the Government. My widowed mother instructed me herself. We read the Bible on Sunday mornings. I wouldn't say she was domineering but she was intense and frail at the same time. And devoted to me. She was a seamstress who made my clothes when I secretly longed for a dress from the store. She lived long enough to see me graduate from high school and become engaged to Joseph. She gave him her tiny diamond engagement ring to give to me. I had no heart for a wedding without her. She missed out on what she would have loved most: grandmotherhood. Joseph's world that consisted chiefly of his father became my own.

It's not easy to live with a father-in-law like mine. To live in a musty house with a brick-colored living room, and dark furniture—a maroon sofa, his old brown armchair and footstool, everything plush, so prickly and warm in summer. He wants nothing changed. "We should have our own place," I murmur sometimes to Poppa. "They're closing more banks," comes the reply. "Mine may be next."

We want a child. I become pregnant and we speak happily of the future. One day at dinner I mention baptism.

"A barbaric ritual!" sneers Grandpa. "Half-drowning an infant so the priest can make some extra change."

"That's unfair!" I say, then turn mute, the Grandpa effect.

The nearest church is miles away. I've seen it, a small, rundown box of a place. Secretly I plan to go there with Joseph and the new baby. Poppa understands my desire as a kind of tribute to my mother.

We call the baby "Michael" after Grandpa's father. The baby is beautiful. I am nervous thanks to Grandpa. He cares only for his routines, especially dinner. I have only a little breast milk for a few weeks. The baby does better on a bottle. He is such a colicky baby. I wish he would let Joseph hold him. Between Grandpa and Michael I am a wreck. Joseph hopes the ceremony will comfort me. Unlike his father, he agrees with me that some Power hovers mysteriously above the State. Neither of us knows exactly how or why. I tell Joseph a little shyly that the highest power may be love. He smiles, embarrassed at too much sentiment.

"Superstition!" thunders Grandpa. He sounds like God himself.

Where can that love be now? Escaped to another world? I think of the Love Room, that mockery, and cross myself. I have never felt so religious. How comforting rituals must be.

I touch the prison mock over my knees and feel the baby sitting in my lap on the bus. Joseph takes him as we alight. He squirms, so I take him back. We walk down a shabby street with deserted buildings. This was a nice neighborhood when I was a child. The church is a simple frame structure that looks like a store. The old one burned down years ago in the wave of church burnings.

Inside there are rows of plain wooden benches. The altar is sort of makeshift, a wooden table covered by a cloth. On it stand two dingy brass candlesticks with short candles that have dripped many times onto the cloth. No one is there. We are on time, so we wait. Then we call out, "Hello! Anybody there?" The vestry door opens. An old priest with a red face and threadbare black robe emerges. He stumbles. We see that he is lame. He smiles and we observe he has teeth missing.

He settles on the altar steps like a dark bird. "What do you want? Baptism? This child is innocent."

He leans over and peers up at me. The alcohol on his breath makes me feel faint. "Now you come here," he grumbles. "I never saw you before. You're too late!"

Joseph and I turn to leave. The priest is pointing at the baby. His eyes blaze.

"Take him away! Hide him in the bulrushes! Leave the country. Leave the planet!"

"That's right. Run!" he shouts. There's a firestorm coming. Pestilence and plague. Look out for the hailstones! Munch on the locusts! A hard rain will fall!" His laughter careens through the empty church and follows us to the street.

We never tell Grandpa. Our children are not baptized. I pray for you my sons. In this cell.

A Guard comes by with a hose. He douses me with a cold, watery disinfectant. My mock sticks to my skin like a sausage casing. Baptism of a sausage. In hell.

"You bathe every day!" marveled Joseph when we were first married. A black circle in a white square lies over my heart. A target. When? When?

In the courtyard workmen come and go with saws and hammers to put up a scaffold. Spectator stands are in place. A prisoner stands in his red-circled mock, hands behind his back. Waits to be shot or hanged. Shamefully I wager with myself which it will be, reminded of days at the lottery office. I can't look. If the man were Joseph, would I die of grief? Are you here, Joseph? I look at the ceiling and call to God. Maybe he is hiding in the cracks. That empty church. Anybody there?

I run away into my head, into my kitchen. I must peel the potatoes waiting for me in the sink. They blink running water out of their eyes and turn to stone. I scrape carrots. They bleed. An onion browning in the pot screams. I pour cold water over it. The steam scalds me. Better to think of a big book with many pages. I'll climb into it and close its covers.

I used to take Michael with me to the library. I liked books, even the ones I could not understand. It upset me when they cut the days, then the hours. People said computers were replacing books. Most computers got sick with some magnetic viruses and had to be turned in. Some new ones were vaccinated but they were expensive. Not many people around us had them at home. Publishers were switching to bookpads, anyway. Portable bookpads of simple information and easy-to-read stories. But books were good to hold! Like a person. To touch. The feel of pages stayed with you. They didn't just disappear.

We take the bus to the library and see a new sign on the door: "Open for Returns Only." The library is closing. I want to cry. No more trips here. The Book Recycling Campaign begins. It will turn books into toilet paper. Instead of visiting the library we go to the park. I am pregnant with Charles and enjoy walking less and less. No wonder you resented him, Michael! It's clear to me now. Too late, like the priest said. You're too late.

We put a few books and magazines out with the garbage. We haven't many possessions so we hide most of our books. A few less wouldn't make us unpatriotic. We take them out of the bookcase and put them into an attic trunk, then fill the shelves with odds and ends, photographs, Grandpa's two tiny cactus plants that I secretly water. Grandpa says they require no water and so should receive none. Rigid and prickly, that was Grandpa, like his plants. They may still be alive. I hope he's right about the water.

Grandpa is upset about moving things around. "Soon I won't be able to find my toothbrush!"

Some people have cartons of books taken away. It almost becomes a contest. The town bookstore closes and converts to a convenience store.

The Government advertises a new Peace On Earth Plan. It sounds like the old Global Pacification Program. People say it will create jobs but I don't see life improving. For the first time I see a beggar in town, a woman pushing a tattered stroller. I give her a dollar and she moves away quickly. Her face is familiar—a mother from school! Soon there are more beggars, drunks, and street people in town. Almost like a city.

Joseph worries about his job. People look at each other warily. Perhaps Grandpa is right. Only your own family matters.

The President appears on television. Every week he gives more bad news and hints at a new solution. "Callow rascal!" shouts Grandpa. He listens to the news station that repeats every twenty minutes—good for short memories. The news changes and nobody seems to care about or remember the old.

The President makes an important announcement. We gather in the living room to watch his hazy image. He talks about mobilizing families for Total Effort. Says a National Honor List will be posted on a special day every six months. Final selections to be drawn by lottery. Sons fifteen and over will be inducted into Military Service, if not already conscripted. Daughters may choose between the Military and childbearing—in or out of wedlock. Underage children (and unwelcome offspring) will become wards of the State in Young Patriots' Homes. Parents will be assigned to Service Camps or wherever needed. "We are democratic!" the President says. "Do for your country, and your country will do for you."

"Your country will do you in, stupid!" Grandpa shouts at the sputtering set. "Five years messing up families! Suppose they take all of you? What will happen to me?"

For once I agree with Grandpa. "It sounds like a disaster."

Suddenly he is coughing and clutching his heart. It's not a heart attack but he begins to fail around that time. A year later he is dead.

They tell us that the greatest honor for any family is to be on the List. The greatest dishonor is an attempt to beg off. Later we hear stories about deferments exchanged for cash or favors. Nobody knows for sure. Who would dare print such things or discuss them openly? We notice that wealthy folk rarely if ever make the List. The poor are most frequently honored. The notion grows that they are superior. People are satisfied that something is being done about the country's problems. We hear a lot of cheering for the President, especially on the radio where he usually speaks.

Two years later our names appear on the List. Michael is happy and Charles is confused. Joseph seems almost relieved, as if he is receiving employment insurance. I feel dread. I remember the day our notice arrived.

Joseph came home from work, kissed me, removed his coat, and checked the mail on the small table. He picked up the letter. He saw the anxiety in my face and tried to joke.

"The Government is thrifty. Four names on one envelope." He read the letter aloud and handed it to me. I kept it with me. I reread it enough times to commit it to memory.

"Dear Members of the State:

I am pleased to inform you of your selection from the National Honor List, the greatest honor for any family in our Beloved Country.

Therefore,

1. Michael A., aged 17, must report for induction into Military Service two weeks from the above date, on Monday, June—, at 9:00 a.m. Address:—.

2. Charles A., aged 10, must report to the Young Patriots'

Home where he will reside, three weeks from the above date, on Tuesday, June —, at 9:00 a.m. Address: —.

    3. Joseph A., aged 45, and Serafina A., aged 40, must report to the Depot Office for assignment to Service Camp four weeks from the above date, on Wednesday, June —, at 9:00 a.m. Address: —.

    Congratulations.

    Hail to our Country.

    General G. H. Q. Gutsby, Commander

The letter is accompanied by four Entry Papers and more instructions.

I wept. Father touched my shoulder. Charles ran to me. "I'll stay with you, Momma," he said.

"Baby! Baby!" Michael taunted.

"It will be hard on the family," Poppa said.

"The country is more important," Michael answered.

"Nonsense!" said Poppa, sounding like Grandpa.

"That's treason!"

"Are you accusing me?" The sorrow in Poppa's voice. You, Michael, heard only the anger and kept silent. A crust formed around you.

    Poppa shouted. You shouted back. For the first time he slapped you. You said we made Charles a sissy and maybe they'd straighten him out at the Home. Charles cried. You left the room. I felt as if my womb had been scraped. I still can feel the hollow.

J.

Birds. When I'm not thinking about Serafina and the past I try to imagine birds. Little gray ones with gentle wings — Serafina birds, maybe nesting in the eaves of my cell. Or ferocious parrots — Joseph birds in green and yellow with jagged beaks that can crunch off a Guard's finger. I imagine eagles lifting me out of here. Before the bank, I worked briefly in a bird store. People lost interest in birds. They no longer survived well. Something about the air. Guard dogs became popular. I try to keep birds in my head and think a blue sky for them. The sky breaks up into clouds falling as bullets that cluster into bombs. When I imagine a bird flying it hits a wall and drops dead. The big ones too. Then I see myself as a bird, safe in a cage. I gasp for breath. I remember that human bird in one of my father's old books—Icarus? "I Care for Us." My own arms flap in waxen wings that melt all over the cell. A diarrhea of wax all over me. What a mess! Can't even think myself out of here.

Michael tears at my heart. Haven't I been a good father? No matter. Something terrible will happen. I feel it in my bunions, in my joints. Arthritis of the spirit. Serafina and I are good people. We were never in trouble before this.

He is innocent! said the priest. Is Michael innocent? Am I such a criminal that my son is preparing to punish me? Do all sons punish their fathers? Not Charles. Not yet, anyway.

S.

Michael—I see you wresting your suitcase from Poppa, refusing his help. Will you ever forgive that slap? I tell him it hurt more because Charles saw you get hit. Poppa is sorry but you are both so stubborn. You clutch the little brown suitcase. Its old leather is faded and dry with crumbly straps. We walk you to the bus stop. You won't let us accompany you further. You hug me. You stiffly hug your father and shake hands with Charles. Your little brother! How cold. We wave from the street. You look ahead. Poppa takes my hand. The three of us go back to the house. Charles is quiet. He knows his turn will come.

"They shouldn't take our children," I complain to Poppa.

"They can't make exceptions," he says. "If serving the country is good for one it's good for all." His certainty is hard and sharp-edged, like a rock. I remind him of Grandpa's views.

"You never even liked my father!" His words are so close to the truth that I weep with anger. I think of running away with Charles. Where can we go? How can we hide from the Government? From our duty?

I sit by the window, child in my lap. "Not my boy!" I say to Poppa. The man is in pain too. He says Charles will be miserable if he picks up on my fears. So in the end I betray my own motherhood. Poppa takes you for a walk. He will repair the damage I've done.

J.

The smell of disinfectant on my skin. It's like a cheap shaving lotion. Again I direct my nose to transform the stink. Sweet honeysuckle climbs along the nature walk. Mostly woods there with a few paths narrowed by foliage, strewn with dead leaves from a leftover season. It's easier than imagining birds.

Charles. He was with me that last day of my fatherhood. I must set him straight.

We can feel the bay a few miles ahead. On the other side lies the ocean that I always feared. My father was afraid I might dare too much if I could swim. I taught myself to float. I made sure that you and Michael learned to swim. Give me credit for that. Credit for a good paternal deed—in a ledger no one will read.

The pond is quiet and familiar. I don't remember seeing ducks. No gang of boys. Serafina now fears being alone too long. We never found out about the broken fence. We stop here.

You pick up a handful of pebbles and throw them in. "Try one like this." I send a pebble skipping over the surface until it sinks. You copy me, try a few times, and succeed once.

Put that in the ledger.

We sit on the mossy bank. "You are starting an adventure," I begin. "We all are. The Government needs us. We are important people." Banalities. On and on. Poor child! I cap it all with, "You will be a good boy and do as they tell you. Make us proud."

"You mean I won't see you or Momma there?"

My heart sinks like a stone in the pond. "There won't be anyone to put you on her knee, and you're too big for that anyway."

You start to cry. So much for good intentions.

S.

I awake early while Poppa is sleeping and go to your room. Can I carry you away, child, even now? I kiss your cheek and return to bed. Then up to make breakfast. The kitchen is solace, the plain center of daily life. The snug inside of a fresh roll. Then you are up, and Poppa. You drink the squeezed orange juice, a fine luxury, and eat your cereal. Your plump fingers clutch the spoon, your face intent on oatmeal with raisins and brown sugar. I follow each spoonful into your mouth as you empty the bowl and show it to me. I smile at the good boy you are.

We walk down the street and board the bus. We ignore the few other parents who are seated with their children.

"When will you visit me?" you keep asking. I press your hand. "Suppose I get sick, Momma?"

"Of course we'll come if you get sick!" I make you a promise. Poppa looks concerned. Well I am your mother and you need assurance. You know I keep my word.

The bus reaches the Armory. What a grimy monster, all tiny eyes with a door like jaws. Unlike Michael entering the recruitment center, you will disappear before our eyes. This new beginning—I detest its cold, murky face, its mouth ready to swallow you. The old Armory, converted to a Young Patriots' Home. How can it be your new home without us? This place we can't even see?

Soldiers stand guard at the iron gate. Beyond it a tall, oaken double door. A boy weeps as his parents plead with a soldier in the sentry booth. The man turns from his computer and scribbles in an outsized ledger. He shakes his head. Parents must say goodbye then and there. The child bawls.

Poppa tries anyway. "Please sir, may we go in with our son?"

The man scowls and taps on a small printed sign that hangs in the window: "Deposit Children Here with Entry Paper." Joseph mutters to me, "Deposit Litter in Wastebasket." The soldier concentrates on his computer.

Poppa holds the Entry Paper near the man's hand. The sentry snatches the form like a goldfish nipping a surface crumb. His crew cut matches the gray steel frames of his glasses that match his uniform. He keeps scribbling on paper and tapping computer keys. Other parents and children arrive. The soldier glances at you. "Step inside!" he commands. We hug you briefly as another soldier grabs your arm and leads you beyond the gate. We watch your little backpack bob up with each step you climb. You look back. We wave at the heavy door closing behind you.

J.

Despite the emptiness of the house, I am content to have Momma to myself. We put away family treasures, framed photographs, some of them from the bookcase, a pair of silver candlesticks, an afghan crocheted by Serafina's mother. My father's leather-bound classics were already in the attic, along with the family Bibles and Momma's few books. We store clothes and debate trifles: where to hide Momma's gold bracelet and necklaces, my two gold pieces; whether to take down pictures from the walls or cover them in place. We decide on the latter.

It goes against me to let a stranger use my bed, so I do not seek to rent the house. It will await our return. A pleasant illusion. As Honorees our taxes are suspended and the grounds are supposed to be maintained.

Unlike Momma, this final week I feel little depression. I relive my childhood, euphoric days innocent of the responsibilities my father held like coins in his hands. Five years free of job worries. Let them close every damned branch and turn the company over to robots. Let the bank burn, money and all. I hear a bell, and like a boy liberated from school I am taking the long, sweet walk home to the warm arms of my mother, to a cool glass of milk and plump, sugary cookies. Surely the Honor List is my release! I lie in bed growing younger and smaller, a good size for a wicker bassinet. In my dreams I am floating in an amniotic sea.

We breakfast in silence. Place the garbage at the back door. Disconnect appliances and lamps. Leave the door of the empty refrigerator ajar. Get dressed. Pack lightly.

In the living room Serafina has shrouded every table, picture, lamp, and chair into a mystery of sheets and rags. Already we are ghosts.

"Maybe we'll return soon." Momma shakes her head. "We'll be together," I say.

She remains silent.

I hook my arms into my backpack and pick up my wife's little suitcase. She wants to carry it.

I lock the door. Serafina looks back.

We board a bus that travels in the opposite direction of the Home. By the tracks a golf driving range that I remembered is now a rifle range. As the bus passes under a walkway, something heavy hits the roof.

"Goddamn kids!" the driver shouts. "Oughta be shot."

Nevertheless it is a blue and balmy morning, a workday. The overhead whir of helicopters makes me uneasy. Serafina clasps and unclasps her hands. I hold them still. "We'll be there soon."

Outside the dingy, graffiti-scratched windows, modest homes give way to a stretch of tenements that alternate with vacant, charred buildings. Two young men are fighting in the street. One pulls out a knife. Other couples get on the bus. They are poorly dressed and carry light luggage and shopping bags. We wonder if they too are headed for the Service Camp. The street fight continues as we pull away.

We travel farther from Charles and Michael and from lives that are no longer whole but fragmented. We reach a stretch of vacant lots and the driver hollers, "Depot Office!" At first there is nothing to see but a little sign with an arrow pointing across the rubble. Another couple gets off, maybe more. A four-story building rises directly ahead like a gigantic brown mushroom with an overhanging roof. The newish structure is distinct from the desolation around it.

It's nearly nine o'clock.

I am going to set down what it was like from that moment when I took Momma's suitcase and half-dragged her along. How right she was to be reluctant. She perspired freely and gasped that she felt unwell as she let me rush her through the opaque glass automatic doors. I found a water cooler. She took a couple of swallows and made a face. I sampled the liquid. Metallic.

The building was spacious and remarkably quiet. Behind a long low extended wall, ten clerks on a raised platform faced the room. Like bank tellers, I thought. People lined before them, carrying forlorn suitcases, cardboard boxes, shopping bags, and ancient grips tied with rope. They patiently waited to deposit their lives in a kind of depressed anticipation, their property exposed like wounds. They were a miscellaneous gathering of faint odors: food, body smell, fragrance, detergent, disinfectant. Even patience seemed to have its smell.

We approached the lines. Three female secretaries seated at long desks behind a metal railing formed a barrier spanning the width of the clerks' wall. To the right of each desk was a turnstile, a number-registering screen in its hub. A large sign in black letters hung above the railing:

NATIONAL HONOR LIST
APPLY HERE

Had anyone ever really applied for the list? The sign must have meant, "LISTEES APPLY HERE." Or "LISTEES REGISTER HERE." Confused and confusing. An inauspicious beginning.

The short lines moved fairly quickly. Though there was no place to sit, my ailing Serafina would soon have her turn. The secretaries wore impersonal expressions matching those of the clerks behind them, and were dressed in identical gray uniforms that matched the walls. Hair—of males and females—was cut almost equally short. Mouths were grimly pursed, like tailors holding pins.

A stout, orange-haired woman of about thirty-five preceded us. The secretary checked through the computer file, handed her a folder fastened with a seal and name printed on the tab. Then she stamped the woman's wrist, pulled her through the turnstile, and pressed a button. "Next!" announced a disembodied voice.

Serafina flinched. With my foot I nudged her suitcase closer to the desk. Attempting to reassure her by example, I announced myself. The secretary riffled through her folders and handed me one. My name was on the tab.

"What is this?" I asked, taking the folder. The secretary seized my right wrist and stamped it.

"Take your chart," droned the same recorded voice. "Go to Number 3. Next!" The mute secretary pointed ahead to the left.

Chart. Number. Like a hospital clinic. As I passed through the turnstile it registered 3015, the figure stamped in blue on my wrist, and showed a sinister-looking photo of me above it. When I held back to wait for Serafina, a Guard prodded me with a baton. He too was wearing gray. I caught my wife's stricken expression. Wary of calling attention to her weakness, why then did I move on with barely a protest? I was a coward. Behold the stigma on my wrist!

From line Number 3 I observed Serafina receiving the imprint and her file. Grasping her suitcase she emerged tearfully from the turnstile. I beckoned to her, she shook her head and walked to line Number 5. We gazed dumbly across line Number 4 until she reached the clerk who took the folder. He stamped it with the letter of a bus leaving for the Service Camp. As he returned the folder I sensed that Momma was inquiring about me. My turn came just as a Guard led her to a door near the end clerk. If we were placed on different buses—what would that mean? Would we be housed together? I tried to calm myself. Surely the Government would not separate us. Service was an honor, not a punishment.

"Sir," I began fearfully, ready to address the clerk as "Your Majesty" if necessary. "My wife is over there in Number 5. Will you please place us together on the same bus?"

The man leaned forward, snatched the folder, and stamped it. "Arrangements have been made," he snarled.

"Arrangements?" My voice curled backward, an ineffectual wisp of hair.

"Go to Exit! You're in the Bus B text. Next!"

I took my chart and fled in pursuit of Serafina. The Guard at Exit cautioned, "Don't run!"

The door opened to a cylindrical metal shaft. A spiral with treads widely spaced pitched steeply around it. Below I could see Momma's head bobbing.

"Serafina!" She looked up, uttered a sound like "A-a-ah!" Hands shot out at the landing, shook her into silence. She continued her descent and disappeared. I rushed down the steps. About halfway, on the narrow landing, a kind of sentry box protruded slightly from the metal wall. A small round mirror, nearly midway up the door, resembled an eyepiece.

"Don't run!" issued a voice from the box, startling me. I tripped and almost fell the rest of the way. When I got to the bottom, a wall panel slid back and a hand emerged.

"Come on!" the hand rasped. I stepped into a dimly lit tunnel. The voice revealed a tall, slender Guard, either an albino or pale from the lighting or having worked too long underground. He mumbled into a walktalk. He noted my chart and held a small flashcard.

"Raise your right hand," he snapped. I did. A blue light from the card glanced off my palm, leaving a luminous imprint that read "B1."

Three vehicles waited ahead. Tubular, with flattened ends, they lacked wheels or windows. Resembling the metal of the staircase cylinder, each bore a name in luminous black letters on its side: "Bus A," "Bus B," and "Bus C."

I glimpsed Serafina peering out of Bus A before the door closed. "There's my wife!" I told the Guard.

"No matter.

"Bus B, Seat One."

"She's on Bus A!"

"I'm talking about your seat, stupid."

He shoved me toward Bus B. I prepared to dash to Bus A when it lifted a short distance from the ground. Whoosh! It traveled out of sight into the tunnel.

Again I was too late. I felt like an insect crawling to my bus. Its door slid open.

"Step up and raise your right hand!" a voice issued from the cavity. I obeyed.

A driver sat at the control panel. He smiled a shark smile. His pale blue uniform reminded me wistfully of the sky we had left. Wasn't blue the color of hope? Something from a book in the attic. "Abandon hope, all ye who enter here." Who had said that? Besides my father?

"My first victim," the driver observed, smiling. "Seat One, over there."

"My wife is on Bus A!" I told the new listener.

"Good for you."

"Are we headed for the same place?"

"Hell, yes! You can't have everything."

Relieved, I ignored his cynicism and put my knapsack at my feet near the door. There were five pairs of numbered seats along the narrow aisle, each molded to fit a moderate-sized bottom. A woman entered, followed by eight more passengers. She lifted her palm in a coquettish salute to the driver who whistled and winked. "B Two." She gave me a searching look and sat beside me. It was the red-haired woman I had followed through the turnstile.

"I'm Moira." She parted her lips, widened her blue eyes ingenuously, and extended her hand, which she made no effort to withdraw until I let it drop. Short hair stood out from her scalp in a frizzy glow. Her expansive bosom rested on arms folded protectively over a worn black alligator bag and a plastic tote.

"Your wife coming?" she asked.

"Her bus left."

"So did my husband's, I think."

The bosom heaved and the low-cut dress revealed a doughy cleavage. I was distracted by the door closing and a little pop! at my ear.

"Sorry," said Moira, fingering her cleavage as if I might have missed it. "I got a gum-cracking habit. Like a kid, y'know? My husband hates it. Maybe he ought to stay lost." Her sudden intimacy embarrassed me.

The bus rocked slightly and the lights dimmed. A soft whooshing sound reminded me of the sea.

"How long is the trip?" I asked the driver.

"Classified info." His neck seemed to puff up. "You in a hurry? Got a hot date?"

He was right. I was rushing to nowhere. Underground.

"I hear it's quite a joint," said Moira. "The Camp, I mean." She smiled, waiting for my response.

"You can have some fun," she went on archly, nudging me for emphasis. "Get me?"

"I haven't heard anything."

"You don't say."

"Not a thing."

"Humph." She shrugged, examined her stubby gilded nails, crossed her legs, and smoothed a stocking. "I always have trouble with stockings. I need a girdle, the old kind, but my husband hates them all, the dog." She smiled. "I used to wear a garter belt, for the effect, you get me?" I moved away, fearing another poke in the ribs. "I wear garters. Just an old-fashioned girl," she laughed.

Moira tugged at her garter through her skirt, then uncovered a mass of heavy thigh. She replaced the hem and laughed. "You can look now."

I was trapped between the wilted bouquet of perfume and the passengers' nervous chatter.

"Okay, this is it!" said the driver. The vehicle rocked gently. Our brief ride was over. He pressed a button. We filed out into the lighted station.

Adjusting my knapsack, I was startled to see a beautiful young woman approaching. She wore nothing but a khaki military cap, gold-braided G-string, and short black boots. Her small breasts were amazingly firm, I thought guiltily, recalling my wife's bosom, disciplined strictly into a brassiere. The woman was carrying our country's flag.

"Welcome to Service Camp 66!" she cooed. I am your Guide." She took our folders.

Moira giggled. "See?" she whispered. I told you it was some place."

We followed the Guide to the end of the platform where a squat door slid open. Out of delicacy I steered Moira ahead of me. The Guide's bare buttocks were unavoidable. At either crest each one flaunted a small tattoo of the flag. Her matter-of-fact bearing made my discomfort seem vulgar. I heard giggles and appreciative whistles from the group behind us. The Guide beamed.

My Serafina! Lost in this strangeness. My wrist began to itch badly. The numbers 3015 were raised. The blue imprint was now outlined in red. My hand began to swell.

The Guard at the door saluted smartly as we trooped through.

The brightness hurt my eyes. Except for the strong white light, everything seemed gray. A high passageway extended from the entrance to a distant wall. Something between a cathedral dome and a railway station with an institutional face. In the center a broad column of steel reached from floor to ceiling. This was the Control Tower, we learned later. It was flanked by a metal partition about eight or nine feet high that hid the area behind it. Narrow outside walks separated the floors which were accessible by four sets of stairs. Identified by the Guide as our bunks, rows of compartments radiated from the walks about halfway around the wall.

On the far side of the dome beyond the partition and facing the bunks, the visible upper portion of the wall was studded with large metal racks, cradling what appeared to be missiles. Ranging from about ten to fifteen feet in length, with snub noses and tails like fins, they suggested gigantic penises. An awesome sight. A movable platform, held in place by upper and lower tracks and vertical beams, was slowly raising one to the top of a row. Along every beam ran a repeated warning in red letters: DON'T ROCK THE CRADLES.

Nearing the steel column the Guide blew a soundless whistle. The smooth facade broke open. A small, thin man with aviator-style glasses and a yellow jacket emerged.

"Do you want them here, doctor?" the Guide asked.

"I don't want them anywhere, but if you insist—"

"Shall I begin?"

"Any time, dear, any time." He licked the cracks in his lips. Behind him ballooned a nurse.

The Guide faced us. "Undress!"

Murmurs issued from the group. "Here?" "Right here?"

"Remove all clothes. Place bags and all belongings on the convoy belt to your left. You may keep toilet articles only. Put them in the bag you will receive. Hit it! Now!"

"This is ridiculous!" a tall woman spluttered.

"Nownownow!" shouted the Guide.

"In mixed company?" the woman asked. "Ouch! I'm shot!" She groaned and tottered, rubbing her chest.

The Guide aimed a pen. "It's just air," she said sweetly. "Come on. We're on a schedule. Hit it!"

"My suitcase!" "My knapsack!" "My watch!"

"Maybe small handbags or plastic bags are okay," she conceded. "Nothing else."

Reluctant, bumbling, floppy odds and ends of shapes, we complied, vainly trying to ignore each other into privacy. I kept thinking of the boy who bumped into me on the street and stole my wallet. That surprise of being robbed.

Gazing down the lumpy slopes of skin to my bunions and hammer-toes, I hated the exposure of my deficiencies. Naked, facing the implacable doctor and nurse, the former with stethoscope, the latter with hypodermic, we were cattle waiting to be probed and punctured. Moo, I joked inwardly to keep up my spirits. With relief, I noted that the needles were disposable. The nurse ejected them into a plastic container strapped to her waist. At least the place seemed sanitary.

At the base of the column a partition slid back. The convoy belt moved our belongings toward the opening. The doctor squinted at me distastefully over his brown moustache, peered into my mouth, thumped my chest, listened briefly for a heartbeat.

"Yes," he commanded the nurse who promptly slapped my arm and jabbed it almost to the bone. She ignored my swollen wrist and hand. She indicated a dispenser of flat packages and barked, "Put on the mock and scuffs. Keep toilet things only in the empty bag. You each get a fresh set in your bunk. Ditch that dirty knapsack, Buster," she aimed at me gratuitously.

I wanted to keep my father's old magazine with an article on our locality.

"Smartass!" snapped the nurse. "What's this, old toilet paper?" She threw the magazine and my knapsack onto the convoy belt. She was intractable. And large.

In the clear plastic case I found a thin gray mock of a synthetic material and a pair of gray plastic scuffs.

"We just wear this?"

She glared. "Next!"

Consoled by my delusion of protest, I became the docile underside of a gray mock and tattooed number. The swelling on my wrist receded.

"Goddamn it! That's a genuine alligator bag cost me twenty bucks at the Salvation Store and it stays with me!"

Moira. Unmistakably. Plump white breasts and dimpled buttocks bobbing as if separately alive. She was actually struggling with the nurse. She shot me a pleading glance before the doctor gave her a slap on the rump. I dashed over to pull her away. Her flesh yielded voluptuously.

The nurse yanked the handbag so sharply that Moira fell beside it on the convoy, which began moving, carrying the woman and her bag toward the column. She shrieked and rolled off while the square hole gobbled up the alligator head and skin. The Guide and the nurse grabbed Moira's arms and led her aside. When they returned she was dressed as drably as the rest of us.

After we all were examined the Guide produced a list that she held close to her nose. Nearsighted and vain, I noted.

"Now to our bunks," she announced.

Desperate, I held to my optimism, half-expecting Serafina to be awaiting me there. Dear lost wife!

Like ten gray slugs we shambled after the little flags on the firm rump, up two flights of skeletal stairs. A tall, muscular Guard appeared, standing with arms akimbo. He wore blue-tinted glasses. His square waxen skull glistened. He wore a khaki athletic support, boots, a kind of ammunition belt, a holster with revolver, and a large ring of keys. He kept his arms in position until the Guide was a step away. He saluted briskly, she saluted, and they repeated their gestures.

"Campers from Bus B," she announced icily.

"Okay," he snarled. "Get lost."

"I'm showing them to their bunks."

"Since when?"

"Today. A new order."

"Says who?"

"Not your business. The highest source."

"They don't issue orders from the Love Room, sweetmeat. Bring me the news on Form DU-IT next time. Until then, jellybean, it's my fucking Sector and I run it."

"The General will hear about this!"

"I bet." He brought his face close to hers and poked her between her breasts. "Listen, blondie, you screw up my promotion and I'll tie your boobs around your neck. Now give me those charts and kiss off!"

The Guide slammed them down on the floor and ran along the walk to the next stairway. Wisps of blond hair emerged from her cap. The Guard glared at the folders and tried to compose himself as his pale skull turned pink. He gathered up the charts.

"Follow me!"

He led us into a corridor at the end of which stood a desk, file cabinet, and cot. Facing them, aligned to the left, were six identical steel doors, marked in black. The first read "Guard." The rest were numbered. All had keyholes but no doorknobs. Like cells, I thought. To the right stood the rear wall of rooms lining the next corridor. From this wall, three rectangular dispensing machines protruded brightly in solid shades of green, blue, and yellow.

"Okay. Lie-nuppin-new-merrical order. B One to B Ten, right palm up. Kay, that's it. Palms down.

"I'm Captain Till, head of this Sector. Everything clears with me, right? You don't piss without my permission, right? Teamwork, and I'm the manager, ha! Teamwork's the ticket here. Eat together crap together. A real family. Right?

"You get Allowance Cards for your services. I give you three cards every week. For satisfactory service." He held up three colored squares. "Green is for candy from the Green Ma," he explained, caressing the green machine, "the blue for soda from the Blue Ma, and the yellow for a pack of cigarettes from the Yellow Ma. We forbid smoking except on the can, so you only get Yellow once. After that you have to fill out a Yellow Ma Form. The place gets messed up with butts and we only like one kind of butt around here." He smirked, making an obscene gesture with his left hand in the crease of his right arm. "We've got a card for that, too. 'Privilege of the Love Room.' But it comes later, when you've proven yourselves good little boys and girls.

"You can use the blue card and the green card seven times. That makes seven sodas and seven candies a week. Everything is sugar-free so we don't keep the dentist busy. Right? You use the Yellow Ma card once, if you want, but the machine won't give the card back like the others do. Kay? The candy wrappers are edible. I mean you have to eat them. They don't taste bad. The soda cans get recycled." He pointed to holes at either side of the machines.

"And you won't have to worry about making babies. It just ain't happenin' down here. So don't expect any dispensers for rubbers or rags. You lucked out, folks.

"And yes. For your own protection, we have an 'I-Zon-U' system—room surveillance. Spot checks. Goes with the central air-conditioning. Everything top-of-the-line in this Camp."

Captain Till removed a key from the ring and inserted it into the first door. It slid back, revealing a tiny room, two bunk beds, two chairs, and a washstand with two packets of toilet articles. "B One and B Two, step forward. Room 203."

"There must be a mistake," I demurred.

Till consulted the charts. "You are 3015, B One?"

"Yes."

"Your roommate is 3014, B Two."

Moira held out her wrist to me and smiled feebly. "Son of a bitch!" she exclaimed. "Well, go fight City Hall."

And she went in.

"This can't be!" I said. "My wife is with me."

"Where?" asked the Captain.

"I don't know exactly. She arrived on Bus A."

"Forget it. Those people are set up already in another Sector. You're wasting my time. General Gutsby will address the new Campers in a few minutes."

"Is this a temporary arrangement?" I suggested, indicating Moira.

"Sure. We're getting your bridal suite ready."

I ignored his sarcasm. "Isn't there someone I can speak to?"

"You have a complaint, Camper?"

"Well—yes."

"You're here five minutes and you want to make trouble."

"No—I mean—"

He sniffed. "I smell something bad. An agitator. Maybe a Terrorist. You better wash off the stink fast."

A hot hand grabbed mine and pulled me indoors.

"What are you doing?" I scolded Moira.

"Take a load off your feet." Then she whispered, "Cut it out! You'll get us shitlisted. And then what, buddyboy?"

While I reflected on her words, the door closed behind me. I tried to pull back the metal, succeeding only in scraping my fingers against the keyhole.

"Now look," Moira cajoled, "there's no point screwing us both up over this. It could be worse—it's a very clean place." She glanced around as if to catch someone spying. "You'll see your wife later. They're just setting things up. Give 'em a chance. You're going to have angina or a stroke at this rate, and who knows what jerks we'll both get stuck with? Loosen up.

You can't fight 'em, so join 'em, what's the harm? How about it, buddy-boy?"

My glare must have been withering. "How about *what*?"

Moira's defenses crumpled like a deflated blowfish. She appeared suddenly old. "Nothin'. Sorry about that," she capitulated. She approached the small mirror over the sink and brushed back the orange bangs from her forehead.

"Geez, I look like a hag."

"You look fine."

She turned quickly and flashed a gold-and-silver smile. "Think so?"

"Yes."

"Then there's hope for us, buddyboy!" She laughed. Obnoxious as she was to me, I preferred her in good spirits. There was enough to feel guilty about.

I did feel guilty. In truth, I felt I was not doing my best to find Serafina. Why had I entered the room? Was I a hypocrite? A coward? I saw my poor blob of protest rising like scum and drawn off. I sat in a chair while Moira put her own toilet articles on the open shelves. Even more than the privacy, I missed having a window. No windows anywhere looking out. Would we live underground—like moles, worms, corpses? Surely we would surface at times. We had to see the sky. The work was obviously secret. An honor! Nearly everything connected with Government was secret. Would we be buried here for five years? Then buried for good? I gasped for breath.

Moira turned around. "You okay?"

"I was thinking about fresh air. Not getting it."

"Better not think too much."

A bell clanged. The small screen beside the sink lighted up. A voice with something of the bugle in it issued from the waving flag framed by a running border of three letters: "GMI."

"Fellow patriots, my fellow Campers: This is General Gutsby." He paused as if waiting for applause.

"Welcome to our outpost of National Honor: Service Camp 66. It is a sacred place. What makes it so? The answer is, You! Yes, you fine specimens of citizens who have offered yourselves, your very lives, made the ultimate sacrifice, for is that not what we mean by giving one's life for one's country? Our mighty nation in its peril has asked you: 'Give us these days, your daily lives. Deliver us from the evil of fear, the evil of war.' And you answered, 'Affirmative!'

"You," the voice continued solemnly, "are the elect. Hallowed be your labors. They will shape the mighty instruments of peace." The flag grew larger and fluttered vigorously.

"What we are making is Peace. An effective Peace that can destroy war. It won't be handed to us from a Blue or Green Ma or delivered to us on a convoy. We have to fight for it, extremely, by our own rules, defend it no matter what the cost, no matter how long the toil. We're talking big money here: we're talking freedom! The biggest jackpot of all! Hail to our country!"

The General's voice receded into a fit of coughing. An unctuous voice took over. I could not lower the volume.

"Thank you, dear General. Fellow Campers, that was our beloved leader, General G. H. Q. Gutsby. I wish to add my word of welcome to you grand new arrivals. I am Mr. Blossom, entrepreneur, known affectionately, I hope—heh, heh, as 'Mr. B.' The camp is a GMI cooperative venture: Government, Military, and Industry. The best team for the best dream. We meet in our Dreamland of Peace!

"Bear in mind that Industry will not be outdone by anybody's sacrifices." By this time, our national anthem was playing softly in the background and grew louder as the man went on. "This is a not-for-profit enterprise. It is supported by the Blossom Foundation to Study War, to which I devote every moment of my free time. Our goal of global peace is in sight. We need your absolute cooperation. We have a Government of Rules, not of men and women. And the Rule of Rules is TRUST US. As our great General Gutsby says, This is a sacred place. More than a mere church, it is our Home Team, sustained by your faith. TRUST US. Without Trust, We Bust! See you in Camp. Hail!" A bikini-clad cheerleader, her image multiplied across the screen and her voice becoming a chorus, chanted musically, "GMI! GMI! GMI!" while turning cartwheels. The TV went blank.

The Blossom Foundation to Study War—hadn't my father once contributed to it?

"Cheerleaders," Moira mumbled enviously. "GMI to you too, Ms. Sunshine. Say," she whispered, "you think they're listening?"

"I guess they tune in from time to time." I tried to sound casual.

"Wonder what those guys look like. Maybe they're giants."

How mysterious they seemed. Faceless, intimidating.

A buzzer sounded and our door slid back noiselessly. Captain Till sat at his desk, his hand resting on the button panel before him. As we stepped out, I saw that all the doors were open. Till controlled them digitally as well as by key. Beneath heavy eyelids he studied us.

"Lie-nupdoublefile!" he blared, rising. The other Campers stepped out. Moira squeezed my hand. She too was apprehensive.

"Toilet!"

Unisex toilets at the rear were clean.

"Supper!" Another lineup.

Everyone followed Captain Till down the stairs. Though we had not eaten since morning I heard no complaints. I wanted to shake the man and scream Serafina's name in his ear. What good would it do? Besides, he had a gun.

We turned right through a gray corridor leading into the cafeteria. Ours was the first group to enter. Inside, again there was gray, punctuated by white tile and chrome at the counter. Several workers stood behind the food containers. We were permitted to help ourselves. I don't recall the meal except as bland and inoffensive. I kept looking at the door, straining to see Momma in one of the next groups entering.

And then she appeared. My beloved Serafina, standing in line with the sheep. Weren't our words bleatings of assent? I had an impulse to cry out, "Ba-a-a, ba-a-a!"

I went a little wild, a fine moment in which I dropped my fear and ran to my wife.

"Go back where you belong!" A husky Guard was prying us apart.

"This is my wife!"

"I don't care if it's your Allowance Card. Get back, creeper." He expected me to crawl.

Captain Till rushed over. "What are you doing?"

The Guard pushed me toward him. "This nutjob is making trouble."

"I want to sit with my wife." I tried to sound calm.

"Get back to your table!" ordered Till.

"That's ridiculous!"

His face reddened. "Oh, a critic already. I'll let it glide since you're newlisted. I'm warning you—we don't tolerate troublemakers. If you don't like your accommodations," he lingered sneeringly over the last word, "there's Form 1040ZZ. It's probably useless, but you can try."

"A strange woman will sleep in my room and you won't even let me eat with my wife!"

"There's a form," he insisted wearily.

"You said it was useless."

"I'll make out a request."

"A form for a form?"

"Okay, wise guy, erase." He squeezed my arm powerfully. We retreated.

The first night was the worst. I tried the door, pushing, tapping, looking for a point that might respond. We were locked in. I paced, then climbed into my berth. Moira's bare leg protruded below me.

"We're gonna die of boredom!" she complained. "I guess we'll have TV programs. We gotta have that. Maybe we can liven things up."

I remained silent.

"Want me to turn off my light?"

"Doesn't bother me."

"Are we supposed to sleep in these damn things?" I heard a softly crunching sound as she turned over.

"Tomorrow we'll have new outfits. The clothing is disposable. Recyclable."

"I always sleep in the raw," she called out coyly.

The next time I glanced down Moira was looking up at me, smiling mischievously, naked.

"See!" she exclaimed. "I told you!"

I turned away, but not before discerning the amplitude of her bosom, thick nipples, the nearly pendulous stomach creased horizontally across the navel. I remember the flesh at her armpits, rounded like incipient breasts.

It was damnable to be trapped and confronted by so much yielding softness. I turned my back. "Good night."

"What a man!" More a cry of distress than a rebuke.

S.

When Poppa and I were separated I nearly died of fright. I hoped and prayed we'd be reunited when the buses arrived at Camp. That didn't happen and they put me into a cell, yes, that's what it was, with this uncouth man Dozie. I was terrified. He tried to set me at ease and told me he had been separated from his wife, Moira. He was sure the mistake would be corrected. He seemed so relaxed about the situation at first I wondered whether he really had a wife. I had never been alone with another man since I married Poppa. I was scared to death. We had always been together and pretty isolated. How could I sleep in the same room with a strange man? If he got offended or angry what might he do? I hated feeling vulnerable. I guess I'd been so all my life but didn't think about it. What a woman takes for granted! And is taken. Born into a style and programmed to continue. My mother her mother. Docile generations. To complement men's aggressiveness? Maybe, except for Poppa. He was kind and sweet. Where was he? I kept wondering. Was he trying to find me?

The Camp: a gray place. A scary, angry place with all those bombs!

Suppose one fell—what would happen? DON'T ROCK THE CRADLE indeed. And the wars that kept popping up! You could fight strangers who were supposed to be trying to kill you. It was better, though, if you couldn't see them, or if you pressed buttons and only saw dots disappear on a screen. Dots had no faces, no families. One could eat the dots or blow up the dots like a computer game. Vent your anger on dots. "Displaced Aggression." I liked that phrase from an old magazine. Something to do with other people's daily living, not mine. Grandpa was a difficult man. Though one ought not speak ill of the dead, I still say he was difficult. I hated washing his handkerchiefs. There was nothing displaced in my feelings about him.

I wondered why my life was being ruined and why Joseph couldn't protect us. Protect me. What a brave try he made in the cafeteria! My heart leaped to him. Yet he had failed. Would he give up? I had faith in him, but what might happen to us here? I hardly slept. What did the name "Dozie" mean? A man who sleeps a lot? A bulldozer? I shuddered. Better not speak much to him.

He let me choose the bunk. I hate heights so I took the bottom one. Soon I could hear a light steady snoring. The familiar sound falling from above eased my mind. It was different from Poppa's intermittent snort! snort! but I could be certain Dozie was sleeping. I realized that I was not going to be attacked. I tucked the white sheet under me. Completely wrapped just in case, I fell asleep hoping Poppa would appear. In my dream he stood at the end of a tunnel, waving. Though I walked toward him the distance between us remained the same. Even in a dream we could not touch.

An alarm woke us at six the next morning. Doors opened. We lined up for the lavatory in crumpled mocks.

Dozie seemed cheerful. He hummed a tune from his childhood. It was nice to hear. But my fear returned. We took fresh mocks, slippers, and disposable towels from a dispenser outside the lavatory. We washed up. The next day showers were added to our routine.

I was not vain about clothes but noted that the new coverings looked just like the old ones. Well that was democratic, in a way. I fondly remembered my school uniform, navy skirt, white blouse, red tie for assembly days. Here it was always assembly. A touch of red would have been nice.

We disposed of our used mocks, slippers, and towels on our way out. In single file, like school, we went to breakfast in the cafeteria. In line we moved small trays past an assortment of cereals, dry toast, pats of margarine and jelly, juice, milk, sugar, coffee, tea. The food was generally pretty good. I liked having choices. The room looked like other cafeterias except that it seemed cleaner than most. It gleamed whitely. Tenders stood behind the counter mostly as observers. Several were Black. It was troubling to think that here also, as Upside, their job opportunities might be restricted.

The air bothered me. It was stale and had a faint odor to it. I tried to remember roses. It was easier to recall the single red rose that Joseph once brought me. I closed my eyes and inhaled its fragrance. The air itself was supposed to be contraceptive. Eerie — but it did mean one less complication to be concerned with.

I saw Joseph following a group to a table. He looked drawn. I waved but hesitated to leave the line. He saw me and tried to signal, then moved to his table. After the meal we followed our Guard to dump garbage and stack trays. We could briefly visit the latrine. Again in line we walked to the factory where we would learn our tasks.

The factory spread out behind the Control Tower. Wherever we moved in the work area we could see the missiles. People called them Pops, short for "Poppas." The name of our own dear Poppa! Those silvery whales (sharks?) in their Cradles looked like trophies of a rich sportsman. At night when I spoke to Dozie he compared them to foil-wrapped salamis. He called them penis shapes and embarrassed me. He said the Government said "fuck you" (his words) to the world with them "just for the Hell of it." He seemed smarter than I thought.

I tried to ignore things but the whole place was obscene. One could get worn down, worn to death. I tried to look on the brighter side. I thought of my mother always worrying about money and paying the rent. Our own tight circumstances at home. Well there were no money problems here. No money! I sensed that it was important to stay well. Medical facilities seemed meager. Even primitive (that doctor and that nurse). In my head I kept my little garden, the few flowers that came up. Yellow and red and orange. Charles crouching over furrows, dropping in seeds. Nasturtiums and marigolds. Straining to aim the watering can just right.

Joseph would rescue us. We'd go back home.

J.

Somewhere on that factory floor Serafina was working. Doing her job, doing as she was told. Like me. I was alert to anything that might help get us out. Away from those bombs. A sea of sharks ready to eat the world. We floated in their midst like sardines. Each canister carried a slogan, like MY COUNTRY ALWAYS RIGHT; ONE WORLD WON; and POPPA STRIKES FOR PEACE (I took "Poppa" as an insult and used the common term "Pops"). Between the missiles there were men in various uniforms shaking the hands of men in dark gray suits. Captions read: OUR COUNTRY IS OUR BUSINESS. GMI. Below the rows of missiles and slogans, fifty gigantic, three-dimensional Formagraphs in living color banded the dome at eye level and papered the metal partition that divided the floor space behind us. The subjects were nude and scantily clad men with women, men with men, and women with women in various sexual positions. The Formagraphs were set in baroque-style gilt frames. These were the decorative objects in the Camp. Beneath the frames ran two consecutive inscriptions: PLAY TOGETHER STAY TOGETHER and REWARDS OF THE LOVE ROOM.

At first the pictures shocked and distracted me. In time I came to appreciate any relief from my boring job and anticipated the weekly change of Formagraphs. These visuals bombarded us with impressions that connected our puny labors with future delights of the Love Room and the thrill of remote destruction.

How dull my job was. They probably gave it to me because of my experience with numbers. I worked at a long white bench in the Lab area, one of several such rows where, a few feet apart, men sat on stools and studied their microscopes. We were to count microbes on slides and note any irregularities. It took me awhile to associate my work with the missiles. In another section, Listees were occupied with explosive devices. The metal casings were manufactured outside the factory. I understood later that the missiles and the explosives, which ironically contained some of the same chemicals as fertilizer, disguised the crucial ingredients: the microbes. In our assembly line we were collecting some emergent types of disease, to be placed carefully into the missile warheads. This delicate work was usually assigned to women, whose smaller hands were supposedly more suited to the task.

What a repulsive project. At first I told myself that the stockpile was used merely to intimidate enemies. The nature of the weapon itself was Top Secret. As days passed and work went on, every missile Cradle remained filled. I rationalized that the disappearing excess was being transferred for storage.

My instructor was a young scientist. He wore a gray mock with a white armband and handled objects with almost sensual gloved precision. He had furtive eyes in a narrow head, partly disguised by his facemask, which he thrust from time to time between me and the microscope. Licking his lips, humming with satisfaction, he would lisp, "Now that's a good batch!" His grotesque enthusiasm suggested a doctor crooning over his patient's decline.

Hypothesis: The business of the scientist is life.

Observation: The business of the scientist is business.

While I knew nothing of biology, the tiny creatures I observed seemed oddly misshapen. Their ruddy tops looked like heads with eyelike recessions and, at times, twisted, serpentine tails. They wrapped themselves around each other in an embrace and then proceeded to chew each other's heads off. The heads grew back almost immediately. For a while the action intrigued me, but the compulsive warfare palled.

The Formagraphs were more interesting. Little by little I found myself looking more carefully at details: positions, faces, expressions, bodies, sexual organs. Graphic enough to amuse but not absorb attention as movies might do. The colors were wonderfully bright and cheery, with outdoor backgrounds—grassy lawns, the seashore, pleasant blue skies. The women kept changing into Serafina.

S.

Each day of the week meant endurance, waiting with the cowlike patience we women are supposed to come by naturally. I began training for a strange job: placing glass vials of liquid into a container, then passing the container to the next worker who carefully sealed it. The vials were handed to me by a Hander. Several of them preceded me on the line. The procedure began up the line with a serious-looking woman. She siphoned the liquid with a kind of large eyedropper from a vat. Moira was a Hander on the line but we barely glanced at each other. The vials were passed through a long, clear container called a Glove Box. This was a sterile area that could only be entered with gloves, attached at intervals to the box. I put my hands into the gloves and took a vial from the Hander next to me, then passed it to the next woman, the Sealer. No one knew exactly what we were doing at first. We were told that the work was important and delicate and women's fingers best handled the materials. As if that made us proud. Hands that stroked a baby's cheek or coaxed milk from a nipple (DON'T ROCK THE CRADLE), hands that could finely crochet. We used gloves at all times in the Lab and dropped them into chutes on our way out. At work we wore sanitary masks and hairnets. It was rumored that an accident had or had nearly taken place. Stories varied. We were permitted to whisper. I felt more nervous than ever.

One evening Dozie told me Poppa had applied for a Form to get a Bunk Transfer. His roommate was Moira. Though Dozie said he too was trying to be reunited with his wife he seemed pretty relaxed about the matter. He could relax about dear Poppa! He saw most of life as a joke.

Dozie worked as a Sweeper, of which there were a few, including several Black men. He walked up and down the Lab aisles with a disinfecting mop and kept changing the wraps for the mophead. He had hated his job at a chicken processing plant, been unemployed for more than a year, and thought of the Camp as an adventure. He considered me a "lady." After my rebuff he made no further advances. I think he found my depression unattractive. Sometimes I exaggerated it on purpose.

Moira looked like a rough sort of person. I began to anguish over Poppa's life with her. Never had I questioned his fidelity. He came home every evening at the same time and we were happy together. But life's frustrations could take their toll. And this was such a sick place.

J.

Having waited vainly all week for the response to Captain Till's request I was in despair. Even a crumb, literally, a transfer to Serafina's cafeteria table would have filled me with gratitude. One morning, when I was feeling especially dismal and the scientist was confirming an unusual feature I had noticed on the slide (some of the creatures seemed to be growing larger than others), we heard a shuffling and coughing behind us. The scientist and other Listees turned around to face two heavy-set men accompanied by a pair of burly Guards in khaki shorts.

Rosy-cheeked (unusual here) and twinkle-eyed, the pair looked as if they had just shared a joke. The taller one was resplendent in a blue uniform, its chest entirely studded with medals. He wore a blue helmet with a large white plume curling over it. I learned that his uniform—feather, medals, and all—was entirely disinfected every day. His gloved hand was linked in the arm of his companion who wore a dark business suit.

The scientist fell to his knees. The other Listees followed his example. He tugged at my ankle. "Kneel, idiot! Don't you know anything?"

I remained transfixed. He sputtered, "It's General Gutsby, dope, and Mr. Blossom, double dope!"

I half-knelt, uncertain whether "dope" and "double dope" indicated the gentlemen or me or served as an inclusive reference.

"All right, all right," purred General Gutsby. "Get up." Everyone rose.

"I love it when they do that," said Mr. Blossom, patting the General's back. "It's so—imperial."

The General frowned. "How are we doing?"

"Fine, General. Just fine."

"Nothing unusual?"

"Nothing."

"No gitches, eh?" said Mr. Blossom.

"No, sir. No gitches or gotchas. Everything on schedule."

"Morale? Absentees? Glummers? Downies?"

"None, so far. All Uppies here."

"Good."

"See that, Gutsie," Blossom exulted, "a happy place for happy people. We're practically running a spa, don't you think?"

"All the time," the General remarked dryly. "This is heavy business, Blossom. It's on my shoulders." He nodded at the scientist. "Good work. Keep it up."

"Up where?" from Blossom. The General laughed, seeming relieved, and the two men walked away, followed by the Guards.

"General Gutsby!" I shouted, pursuing the four men toward the Control Tower. The Guards whirled. The General cast a disdainful backward glance and followed Mr. Blossom through the door.

"I must speak to the General!" I hollered at the angry faces.

"Have you filled out a form?"

"My wife and I—we've been separated—a terrible mistake—"

"Shut up and go file a form!"

The shorter Guard poked his companion. "He doesn't know when he's well off."

"The General—"

"Fill out the damn form!"

"For Captain Basket," the taller one smirked, "Captain Waste Basket." The men laughed and disappeared behind the Tower door.

The scientist was tugging at my ear and screaming into it, "Maniac—what are your doing?"

"Ow!"

He let go, removed his gloves, dropped them down a dispo chute, and took a fresh pair from the dispenser beside it. Obviously he feared receiving germs more than spreading them.

"I want to speak to the General about my wife."

He was quivering. "What's she done?"

"We're in different cells—I mean rooms, and—"

"I'll have to report this." He took a pad of white paper from his pocket and began to scribble.

"I meant no harm."

"Idiot!" he snapped. "The General and Mr. Blossom—the top men of the whole Honor List project—here they are, troubleshooting for a few months on their National Tour, rating Camps, putting us near if not at the bottom of a List. I can just see the report on the President's desk. And you, you anarchizer, pulling down our ratings and getting us into a vat!"

"A what?"

"A vat—trouble—don't you understand anything, dummer?"

He continued writing, then crumpled the paper, put it into his mouth, pulled it out, and pulled off his fresh gloves, stuffed the paper into a glove finger, and tossed the gloves down the chute. Anxiety furrowed his expression. He wasn't a bad fellow. Just didn't want trouble. Suddenly I could relate to that. I heard my silence like a man soiling his pants.

S.

Maybe you were foolhardy in the cafeteria Joseph. In my eyes you were brave and romantic, risking your safety to reunite us. Dozie joked about your action. Now I think he was jealous. I worried all the time. About you and Michael and Charles. My stomach often hurt. I didn't complain. If I were sent to a nurse or doctor, what might happen? Everyone seemed to feel this way, scared to be sick, maybe just scared. I still wondered if Dozie might try something when I fell asleep. He had a way of looking at me at bedtime. His eyes seemed to open wider. I saw that they were blue, dark, but really blue. Funny how long it took me to see that. Was I afraid to look into his eyes, afraid of what I would see? An image of myself? But he didn't approach me. I guess I was boring. I figured he'd be glad to be rid of me.

J.

Daily I asked Captain Till about the forms, daily he replied, "Negative." Two weeks passed. My optimism was draining away. Everything bothered me and being underground was not the least of it. I felt the need to let off steam. Till regarded me as a burr caught in his boot. One day, after my usual question, he took me aside and advised tersely, "Don't call me, I'll call you." His cheek was round with candy.

"Listen," he confided, "you'll get a screw in if you behave yourself. I don't blame you—your roommate isn't my type either. A real cow but what the hell, close your eyes and think of a doughnut. Not the jelly but the hole. Ha, maybe both. Anyway, be good and a couple more weeks gets you Privilege of the Love Room."

"I'm not interested."

"You a unique or something?"

"I'm not a eunuch. I just want my wife."

Till chortled. "They ought to lock you up."

"I am locked up."

"Funny guy. Write your own material, eh? You don't understand about the Love Room. I could—" He checked himself. I held my breath.

"Hmmm." He rolled the candy wrapper into a ball and popped it into his mouth. "Save your Candy Cards. They might come in handy." He dismissed me.

The whiff of bribery! Till was human after all. From then on, I ate no candy and, for good measure, drank no soda. A nonsmoker, I easily retained my Cigarette Card.

Till avoided further conversation with me. We heard later that one of the Guards had been removed—to where?—for withholding cards from

Listees. The rumor was unsettling. Undeterred by Till's aloofness, which I read as discretion, the prospect of bribing him to see my wife obsessed me.

On Monday evening, our MED (Mail Exchange Day for sending or receiving letters), Till gave me this.

> Dear Father and Mother:
>
> I'm feeling fine. The food is pretty good. Some nice-looking girls around. Things will get busy soon, so don't worry if you don't hear from me. I have my own rifle. I'm good at target practice. They're pretty happy with me here. We learn bayonet, laser, and flame-throwing and other kinds of self-defense. Maybe a Military Service career lies ahead for me.
>
> Hope you are both well. Hail to our country.
> Love and kisses,
> Michael

At first I was overjoyed to have your letter. If only I could discuss it with your mother. After reading it many times, memorizing it, I passed it on to her. Like us, you were permitted to write one hundred words once a month. I counted your words. Even with the closing and salutation, the number fell short. How I hungered for each syllable! Children don't understand, which is why they are children. Besides, you apparently had not received my letter. Did you feel abandoned? Mail delivery here was worse than Upside.

"Nice-looking girls." Assigned to your station? Whores, most likely. And you only a boy! Had you ever—? Probably. Hasty growth, so different from when I was young. Profits to be made. Earlier and earlier. Life racing to the grave. People tumbling in pell-mell. Younger replacements to buy and serve and be sold. Maybe you already had a secret existence. We should have spoken more. Father to son. Had I been like my own father, after all, busy putting food on the table, keeping the family intact, keeping the wild dogs of life at bay? "Hail to our country." The salute found on official documents, in public speeches. I thought of General Gutsby and

recalled hearing the greeting sometimes Upside. A sign of youthful enthusiasm? A required military form?

Your childish closing reassured me. I who had fostered your inde-
pendence—you must have read this as indifference—now feared the
stranger you might become.

Surely "nice-looking girls" merely indicated adolescent interest in sex.
Erotica sloshing around me like a sluggish toilet made me overly anxious
for you. I doubted your intellectual needs were served any better than ours
were by our single channel on TV. Everybody watched including me most
of the time. Moira never missed a minute of the three hours offered each
night and extensions on weekends: news entertainment. Enemies threatening us ceaselessly everywhere. Surveys of catastrophic weather, empha-
sizing the woes and perils of daily life Upside. Stories about sex, murder,
patriotic war exploits. Violent sex cartoons, war cartoons, salacious misery
talk shows, advertisements for the Love Room, inspirational interviews
with happy Campers, announcements by voluptuous women, handsome
men, and occasionally by General Gutsby and Mr. Blossom, both now visible. Sometimes nature programs soothed us with visions of the sky, of
grain fields and mountains, rivers, animals. But the real sky—no one knew
when we would see it again. The Camp was becoming our animated
tomb. The word "catacombs" popped into my head but there was no book
in which to look it up.

I gave Till Michael's letter for Serafina. For the most part Sectors were
forbidden to communicate with each other except through Guards. As far
as I knew, the Love Room was the only exception. TV, potentially cohe-
sive, served chiefly to subdue and control. "A people united will never be
defeated." I heard that chant by protesters in my youth. "Meddlesome
fools!" my father would observe. "Terrorists!" the Government screamed.
Had they all been murdered? Exiled? No big protests in recent years. No
real newspapers, either. Only tabloids featuring scandals, horoscopes, ad-
vice. TV back home was merely a fuller, somewhat tamer edition of TV at
the Service Camp. My father had probably been right to discourage its
viewing.

Though personal rivalries flourished among Guards and Guides, we took no group pride in our Sector. Rewards were strictly individual. I assumed punishments were too.

Sometimes on my job, seated on a stool at the Lab bench, I felt myself suffocating. Despite air conditioners and adequate lighting, we couldn't escape the fact of living underground. People looked pale. Even the Blacks in the Camp seemed ashen. A few Asian-looking Listees were there, also pallid. I wondered about the contraceptive air. What else might they be doing to us? Thoughts of Serafina with another man tormented me.

I lay in bed remembering weather. I conjured up my father's radio with its weather reports and forecasts. How I longed for clouds, rain, a change in temperature. The bedroom air conditioner Serafina and I used to have, set at "constant cool" during those few hot weeks when we turned it on. What blissful power to turn it off.

The negative news about weather Upside: edited reruns, most likely. All those catastrophes implied we were fortunate, safe, we astronauts in reverse, housed in our subterranean capsule. I imagined plants, their shapes and textures, their colors and fragrances. Serafina—her freshness, always—somewhere between soap and lilacs, like spring. I tried to reject thoughts of her. Too much loss and frustration.

Plastic orchids banked the entrance to the Gymnasium, teasing reminders of its weekly function as the Love Room. The blossoms were regularly dipped into disinfectant. Air refreshers wafted floral-type fragrances around them. In time I found those synthetic odors noxious. They were lies. We were cultivating a sinister garden of microbes. They lay on the slides beneath microscopes or on the missile-cradling walls. We were gardeners of death.

Cemeteries above us—we lived below the dead! The dead from illnesses, accidents, plagues, wars. The dead from grief, suicide, murder. The angry, roiling dead who did not want to die, the gentle dead troubled by our infestation. We were a new kind of worm to them, boring holes in the earth beneath their rest. Violent worms, following paths of mining drills and wells, taking taking taking from the earth, giving nothing back except waste.

The Camp was set at a cool temperature to suit the underground project and its bombs. I longed for a single hot day. A scorcher. Serafina bringing lemonade to the porch in a glass pitcher, ice cubes rattling, slices of lemon floating among them. Michael and Charles vying to drink the faster. Would the sun ever expose our folly? Or would it just hate us and burn us out. Maybe burn itself out too, like a madman plucking out his eyes. "If your eyes offend you"—how did that go? We were like those new buildings, windowless to foil young vandals. Buildings that got sick with recycled air. My mind struggled to reach up and out of this place, a weed breaking through a paved road. I needed light and natural air, even our damaged variety. Ached for them. I needed air, not a plastic floral spray. Sky, not its image on TV or a wall painted blue.

S.

Dozie picked up Michael's opened letter, slipped under our door. I sat on my bed to read it. A career aiming a gun! My son shooting flames at human beings! What were they making of you, dearest Michael? I should have protested that Letter of Selection for the Honor List. But to whom? My practical questions that kept me from action. Remember the goldfish we had? Overfed by mistake it ate until it burst. Accepting, accepting. Like me.

Why can't Poppa get us out of here? Was he trying? The question pained me. I really meant was he comfortable with Moira. People in isolation could be weak. I was understanding much more about life.

Dozie was kind. He didn't seem to miss his wife. I never flattered myself that it was me. He was simply another type of man, an ordinary man.

Not like Poppa. I thought of him with Moira at night.

Suppose he got bored, or liked her? She seemed brazen. Might Joseph be unfaithful? I wanted to hide myself under the sheet, shroud myself in it. Why must he be the one to apply for Form 1040ZZ? Why not me? Why should he receive our letters first? Is this what it still means to be a woman, second in everything except the kitchen or the Service Camp assembly line that seems to have no beginning or end?

Dozie saw me weeping and took my hand. I did not pull it away.

J.

I was frantic with desire for Serafina, to hold her, to be held. How much of loving is childlike. Consoling touch, hugging, tenderness. Gazing across the cafeteria tortured me. I developed headaches and was permitted the relief of aspirin. My productivity, I thought bitterly, must be maintained.

At last my steadily accurate work gained me Privilege of the Love Room. This was a Saturday night visit to the Gymnasium, converted weekly for the purpose. The Gym was used for brief exercise drills. It also had several joghoppers, walkuppers, and weightlifting equipment. Appropriate that our exercise machines went nowhere and the weights were called dumbbells.

I asked Till if Serafina also had earned the Privilege. He ignored me. As the prospect of ever receiving Form 1040ZZ dimmed, I longed for that fleeting reunion.

At first, in theory, only Guides and Guards were to be "visited." Perhaps this was intended to depersonalize sex, bond workers to the State. Have us associate pleasure with it rather than with individuals. Another way to keep workers apart. In the Love Room GMI was supposed to gratify personal needs, stimulated and advertised by the seminudity of its agents. If the original rules were observed, my "Privilege" might have been to view Serafina's intimacy with a Guard. Of course she would never do such a thing. The growing excess of demand over supply had led to a modification. Thus Love Room behavior was now entirely "free," offering a kind of safety valve. Yet the Room sounded more like a Circle of Hell as wildly imagined in old books and paintings. I was tempted to avoid the place entirely.

• • •

You're a screwy bastard," Moira announced one evening. "Everything's so serious with you." She leaned farther back in her chair, raised one leg, and rested her foot on the sink, affording me an unobstructed view of her luxuriantly haired pubic area. I was no longer shocked. My seduction had become her evening's sport. Naturally combative, failure had only whetted her appetite.

"It's a big joke, buddyboy! Here I am with you and there's my dopey husband with your wife. It coulda been worse. I coulda been locked up with him!" She laughed.

"I sat up in my bunk. "Serafina's with your husband?" "Dozie. Yeah. Cross my heart. His brother's a deaf mute so he's good at signing. Like you have to be good at something, right? So I learned from him."

"You waited till now to tell me?" I was furious.

"Well after the cafeteria jazz when we first got here you seemed so excitable—I thought I'd better keep my mouth shut."

"To protect me, no doubt."

"C'mon," she cajoled. "We can all use a little protection." She drew her raised leg toward her. With her fingertips she delicately massaged the long vein marking her inner calf.

"If your husband put in a request for Form 1040ZZ," I said, trying to control my bubbling feelings, "it might expedite matters. For both of us."

She cast a pitying look. "Wise up already. Form 1040ZZ is a phony. Maybe Till made it up. Anyway, cookie, I don't buy it."

"Wouldn't you switch—if you could?"

"Who knows? Maybe I would if I could, but I can't."

She smiled archly, exposing her upper gums. This was too much. "What kind of a person are you?"

"Want to find out?" She fluttered her eyelids.

"Your husband may be sleeping with my wife. He may have raped her!"

"I should have such luck." She waved her raised knee under my nose. "Don't worry. We can't make babies, if you're worried about bastards. You know it's in the air, maybe the French fries too. Who cares? I'm glad I won't be getting the curse every month."

"Damn it!" I exploded. "You don't believe in anything."

She raised her mock to her hips. "Cut the crap," she snapped. "What are you crabbing about? The food is okay and there's plenty of sex to go around, if you're breathing. What's your gripe? Leave the driving to the big shots. That's their job. You're looking for trouble."

Her knee enraged me. I needed to break its insolent rhythm. I raised my hand and slapped her flesh so that her foot flew off the sink. Leaning over to dodge another anticipated blow (which she might have welcomed and I had no wish to bestow), Moira lost her balance and toppled over. She began to wail and pound the floor.

"You're a fink! A goddamn fink! Get away from me! Don't touch me!"

Whatever a "fink" might be (I vaguely recalled some connection with the old labor unions), I realized she was deeply hurt.

Kneeling beside her I babbled apologies. I had never struck a woman before. The brutal action unnerved me. When I touched her shoulder gently she grabbed my hand and plunked it on her crotch. In pulling me down she nearly dislocated my arm. Her other hand clutched me to her.

Shall I blame our common situation? Distress? Proximity? Can pity be an excuse? I did feel sorry for Moira. My rejection must have humiliated her even more than the slap. Or was I too weary and confused to exercise my usual handy moral judgment?

Untrue, I admitted reluctantly, that I felt only pity. My body was throbbing like some feral creature, unsheathing for both of us to see and for her to manipulate. We grappled on the floor like ravenous dogs wresting from each other a kind of release. I pinned her arms back and felt my rage ebb from me as she moaned softly discreetly this loud bawdy woman this cushion of shuddering comforting flesh under me.

Serafina. I had to be with you or die. Find expiation in your embrace. Lost fidelity—like lost chastity. Either or. No middle space. Did I want to use you as a purgative for my soul (whatever wherever that might be)? My brains were dissolving into porridge. Turning from heartbreak, I turned to Moira, using her too.

S.

Dozie was being kind. He let me speak about Poppa. He was the first man since Poppa with whom I had a personal conversation. In private. What choice was there now? No church, no chapel with a minister to confide in, not even a drunken priest. I vaguely remembered robust clerics in my childhood, men with families, with spirit. No psychologists either here and few Upside these days. Out of favor with the Government and nobody could afford them. Anyway, people were afraid to tell secrets somebody could use against them. I used to have my mother to talk to. She taught me to play the piano. It was fun to play for her, feel her delight in my performance of even the simplest piece. I never touched the instrument again after she died. Joseph and Grandpa didn't care much for music anyway.

Had I selected my homemaker's role or had it selected me? "Count your blessings," my mother would say. I kept reviewing them like a catechism: Poppa, Michael, Charles. People were the answer, weren't they? I looked outside myself and there you all were. Sometimes I wondered what was inside, there just for me.

J.

"You look crummy," Moira observed one evening as The Horror Show ended on TV and I lay quietly in my bunk. The Sex Show was beginning. Maybe another dose of group sex like last night.

"Thinking about your wife, huh." Her tone was disappointed.

I turned over and glimpsed a nude woman moistening her fingers with her tongue. She lay between a reclining man who held his erect penis and another woman fingering her clitoris. Moira switched off the set.

"You want to lay your wife," she persisted.

I wished she'd stop talking.

"You ought to see her in the Love Room."

"What do you mean?" I sat up quickly.

"She got the Privilege like you and me. You can hook up with her there." She was gauging my reaction. "I'm gonna try the place next Saturday night. It's supposed to be very democratic inside," she went on. "Screw anybody you like. Real relaxing. You don't want to miss out, do you?"

She was seeking an answer I couldn't provide. "Like I said, it's democratic."

"If I could get a message to Serafina about it—and you could meet your husband there—"

"Thanks a million. Hah, I just might give that dumb bastard a break."

"Perhaps he and I could change rooms—for awhile—"

"You for real? You got more nerve than brains, I'm sorry to say," she added, softening the insult. "They'd lock us up." Fortunately she was pragmatic.

"Did Till give you a room key?"

Puzzled at first, she squinted at me suspiciously. "That's Enemy talk. I thought they got rid of the Terrorists."

"When did you last open the door and take a walk?"

"Who wants to roam around? What's to see? I wouldn't mind a little window-shopping but that ain't in the program, buddyboy. They gotta keep order, for crap's sake."

"Check the number on your wrist. Check your uniform. We're prisoners."

"Cut it out. You'll get us vatted."

After a minute of glum silence she capitulated. "I'll get a message to your wife, if you want."

Her defeat touched me. "Thank you." She turned the TV back on.

But she couldn't let go. "What if your wife didn't get the Privilege?"

"Well she did," I snapped. "You told me." Crumpled, Moira sat mutely watching a nude chorus line of smiling men and women, tipping their hats.

"Blossom," General Gutsby said as he neared my work post, "we ought to change the name of the Love Room."

Mr. Blossom dropped his companion's arm and faced him. "Why?"

"Too sentimental. Love," he sneered. "Just hormones."

"Whore moans?"

"It's a pain in the ass. Sometimes a lovely pain, I'll grant you."

"Feelings don't bite," Blossom admonished. "Everybody has them, even you. You're a regular stewpot of feelings!"

"Always with the food talk. You need to diet."

"You sure can hit the vulnerable flank. Everything isn't a war, you know."

"Spare me the philosophy. We're talking about a name, just a name. What about 'Service Room' or 'Service Station'? Something like that."

Blossom shook his head. "Sounds like a fuel pump."

"Fuck! It fits. Fuel the body. Oil the nuts and bolts, as it were. Get it?"

"Hmm," said Blossom. "Especially the nuts."

Gutsby seemed exasperated. He poked his companion with something like a riding crop.

"Are you incapable of being serious about anything except takeovers? Or lunch? Or my sun lamp? Gitches keep growing no matter what the reports say and we'll have to move on in three months to the next Camp. Hell knows what we'll find there. This isn't the Gutsby and Blossom Comedy Hour, you stupid prick. We're running the country!"

He smacked his palm with the crop. Fearing he might hit me for emphasis, I cringed over my microscope. The two men were close by and seemed oblivious of me.

"Don't forget the President," Blossom mumbled.

"That joke? That platitude with an attitude? Living in his palatial bunker with the rest of his Appointees? You've dealt with him, Blossom, so you know better. Unless both of you need to have your brains lipo-suctioned."

"I wouldn't exactly—"

"I fucking would! Exactly." Gutsby struck the crop on the counter. My microscope trembled.

"You get so tense," murmured Blossom. He took the General by the arm and tried to move him away. "There could be spies." He glared meaningfully at me.

"What a jerk-off you're turning out to be."

"I'm afraid you're going to pop, Gutsie."

The General's tone softened. "I can pop in the Love Room."

"If something happened to you—"

"Nothing would dare happen to me. The Terrorists are done for. Ever since they tried to blow up the whole damn Government and it went broke with those crazy security measures and cute little military diversions all over the freaking globe. 'Focus!' I used to tell the President. 'Focus!' But did he listen? Lucky we were around to take charge and keep the dummer in place. He can relax, now that we turned the rest of that electoral circus into a lottery. Who was voting? Nobody! It's us or anarchy. Any jackass can tell you that."

His words struck me in the stomach. I felt nauseous. Like my father I had avoided politics entirely. Playing dead! I had voted once to assert my coming of age. After that, the process seemed a ritual exchange of rascals. Everything corrupt. When the lotteries began, it didn't seem strange. In a way it felt more democratic. Everybody who paid to be in it could win it. Nearly everything became a lottery—local, state, and federal offices, including Congress and the National Honor List. So for this catastrophe of my life I could in some measure share the blame.

Gutsby hit the counter again with his crop. My microscope shuddered. "I'm giving my guts!" he shouted.

Blossom smiled. "Now *you're* punning."

"You're a contagious disease." The crisis had passed.

"The old order is dying a natural death. Lingering, but withering away. Remember unions? Remember the Church? Terrorists are terrified. Ha!"

"Families, too." Blossom was getting into step. "They're useful for the time being. A little sprawly, so the plants get cut back. We don't want them taking over the whole fucking garden."

"Downsize the plants," Blossom ventured.

"Zactly. You're tuning in."

"It's my wavelength!" Blossom clapped the General on the back and off they went, followed by the two Guards.

Everything offended: the cradled missiles, the Formagraphs, my work, the entire system bound me in a dreary obscenity at the core of which, arm in arm, stood General Gutsby and Mr. Blossom. The rest of us were no better than slaves.

How could a slave be a National Honor Listee? Honor indeed. Attractive packaging for hostages. Imprisoned probably for life. No wonder G and B spoke so freely. It didn't matter. We'd never go home.

I needed air, fresh air. An emergency case. Serafina and I had to leave here, rescue our sons, our family.

My hand itched and I scratched it raw. I wanted to slice off the number with a razor, burn it away with a laser. The Camp had put its mark on me. Both my hands should be cut off. They made death.

I imagined eyes, unblinking eyes everywhere. I remembered pulling back the eyelid of my dead father when I hoped he was still alive, and watching that stiffening lid refuse to close. I closed it, worrying, Now I have made him really dead. What would he have thought of all this?

S.

Dear Mother and Father,

I have my first blue stripe. It's great. This is how we count: 1–5 Enemy kills, one blue stripe; 6–10, two blues; 11–15, three blues;

16–20, one silver; 21–25, two silvers; 26–30, three silvers; 31–35, one gold. I met a man with two golds. Sixty-nine knockouts. In three months. Not many women doing this, but there are some and they say there will be more. We get special privileges with the stripes. Promotions too. Thought you'd want to hear the good news.

Hail to our country.

Michael

While Dozie watched TV I sat on my bunk rereading the letter. Already my son was killing! Who? Why? Where was he? "Hail to our Country"—where was the love? Michael and other boy-men becoming death machines. If one man killed sixty-nine how many lifeless bodies lay on either side? How many children? Who was threatening you? Us? The bombs—Pops—where did they disappear to? Those quick TV news flashes about "peacemaking expeditions"—were you there? What were the women soldiers like? I was tired, tired of decades of Enemies encircling us. Of Advisers sent to keep peace by making war. Perhaps my father-in-law was right to seek isolation. But it didn't protect us. We were here.

Michael, in your childish intense handwriting I searched for the new young man with "special privileges." Did the Military shred your innocence by day? Creep under your sheets at night to steal what was left of it? My wrist itched terribly. When I was upset the numbers got a little raised and outlined in red. Dozie was lucky. His never bothered him.

He sat beside me, thick fingers lightly stroking my hand. I could have wept. Instead I gently withdrew it.

J.

I was to meet Serafina at nine o'clock Saturday night in the Love Room, thanks to Moira. Never assume a spirit is crushed. Wait for the pulse to return.

The Love Room. Steam valve. Dumping ground for irrational impulses. Freedom co-opted by the State. I peered into the mirror, aware that smart men risked others and fools risked themselves. Had I grown rash with longing for my wife? I had food, shelter, dull but steady work, a position secure for five years. A lifetime! Moira for company, preferable to solitary confinement. Momma and I were physically safe. Resigned to the knowledge that Form 1040ZZ, of doubtful existence, would probably never arrive. If my wife and I could meet Saturdays in the Love Room, why be greedy? I wondered what the place would be like.

Poor family! Already the distances lengthened. Paltry letters. And we still had not heard from you, Charles. Rules became stricter. We were no longer permitted to write letters. Breach of security. A breach of nature not to! You and Michael would get monthly bulletins from the Camp regarding our health. We received letters to keep up our morale. For the sake of production. That was not hard to figure out. Was there something more sinister too? I remembered Gutsby's words about the family. Contemptuous. Did the writing restrictions enforce some stupid new economy measure? The mail load was cut to a trickle. The post office system too was corrupt. People were pocketing its funds. Was there another reason, something vaguely menacing that had to do with the microbes in the Lab?

So many times I told myself that a good father would try to rescue his child from the Young Patriots' Home. It was an orphanage! I was diminishing into a caged laboratory animal, a mouse fed and serviced for a deranged experiment. Dangerous to be human. To be a man.

S.

"You ever been with another man, kid?" Dozie looked at me strangely. I felt as if my breasts were bare.

"I mean before you got married."

"No."

"Not since?"

"Never."

Time was making him bolder. What would he do next?

"Ever get curious?"

"Why are you asking such questions?" I was getting bolder too.

He laughed. "I'm not making a move. But if you change your mind, I could help you out."

How trivial physical intimacy seemed to some people.

"We have more TV now," I said. "You can watch all evening."

He would not give up. "When you see people doing something, don't you feel like doing it yourself? 'Monkey see, monkey do?' "

"I try to think for myself."

"We're not talking rocket science here. Anyway, it's too bad. I really like you," he said quietly. The matter rested.

Dozie appeared otherwise content with his situation. After his year without a job he was pleased to have steady work again. Many Campers had been unemployed, some for years. The Honor List helped with that problem. How I longed to discuss it—anything—with Poppa. Dozie might have gotten bolder with more conversation. Maybe I was too careful. Anyway I didn't need his views. Soon I'd see Poppa! We would be reunited in the Love Room.

I thought of our wedding night at an inn by the bay. A blue room with a homemade quilted bedspread. Awakening to gulls in the cool spring morning, breathing the fine sea air, Joseph looking at me in my long white nightgown, sort of sheer. I was embarrassed for him to see me, a little proud that my body was nicely proportioned. He was deliberate. No roughness or clutching, he knew I'd be frightened. What a meek little bird I was. Not like the gulls. More like a sandpiper scurrying along the shore. In bed he leaned on his elbow, stroked me with his other hand. Everything slow, watching my reactions until I felt myself yearning for something un-known. How I loved him, would have served him and his father without question, on and on. That was what I felt then. During the ride back to the house in his creaky old car newly purchased and soon to be given up, even in my bunk as Dozie watched TV I kept thinking I am lucky to have loved. Lucky to have been loved no matter how many strangers slept in my room.

Yet I felt grateful to Dozie for his blessed sign language. Feeble advances could not bother me. For a time nothing could.

J.

It was Saturday night. I walked with Moira toward the Gymnasium, which had disappeared behind a big, red-lettered sign at the door: LOVE ROOM. As we approached the end of the single line, I searched for Serafina. At last I saw her standing in front of a man whom Moira identified as Dozie. My wife was wearing a pink mock—I had not noticed it on Moira. Mine, like the other men's, was pale blue. Trite labeling for those who had made it to the Love Room. What a critical wretch I had become.

I took Serafina's hand, Moira stepped into her place, and I led my beloved to the end of the line.

"Quiet! Single file! Touching only!" a Guard advised. I pressed my lips to my wife's ear, kissed her, and whispered over and over, "Dearest one." Saying the words, so long deferred, seemed to heal me, subdue my rage and despair. Her voice softly at my ear assured me that Dozie had behaved well. She shared my anxiety about our sons, hated Michael's personal danger and the killings, imagined Charles was ill. She was desperate to see you, lost boy. My mention of escape seemed to alarm her, yet I knew she would let me decide.

How ignorant we were of each other's lives at the Camp. Though Moira had pointed out Dozie, I had never before seen him up close. I had pictured someone of medium build, like myself or more slight, someone Moira could dominate. But instead the man was large, blond, handsome in a brutish sort of way. Serafina might find him agreeable. Odd that she did not question me about Moira. Was she being less considerate than discreet? Balding, paunchy, weak, deluded by my self-righteous morality, I had given in to Moira as easily as a fruit fly. Dozie was like her. I had to rescue Serafina, my family, retrieve my self-respect.

We reached the door. It opened. We caught a whiff of sweetish air and the rhythmic sounds of a drum. Serafina held my hand tightly.

Inside the small red anteroom we joined several Campers waiting before a scarlet satin curtain. I noted with distaste the pair of plastic vases marked GMI and filled with more fake purple orchids. Something tawdry about the scene, yet I was taken with the quiet, almost hushed tones, the ambience of serenity—or docility—despite the impassioned colors. The drumbeat, the voices rumbling behind the curtain merged with the rush of blood through my body.

In the reddish-blue light my wife's eyes seemed mysterious, almost malevolent, although she smiled. I felt a bit giddy, starting to enjoy the sweet narcotic haze. The room became a subtle pressure chamber from which we awaited release. Everyone looked attractive.

Without reluctance or even surprise we all obeyed the command to undress. As we crowded together to enter the Love Room, a young man behind Serafina pressed against her. She merely turned around—did she smile? Taking her arm roughly, I led her in.

The dark floor was alive. A mass of reddish, serpentine flesh, coiling and writhing on mats, moaned, quivered, and thrust in the dimness. I did not mind the loud drumbeat. A hand pointed to an empty mat. We sat down. I felt remote. There I was, finally with the dearest of women, whom an unfamiliar self seemed to have invaded, a self indistinct from the moaning, sighing, giggling, struggling bodies pulsing with the relentless rhythm of a drum. Moths reverting to caterpillars.

The two voices were unmistakable. As in a dream the pair approached, naked as the rest of us. Democratic. Unaccompanied by Guards who might very well be performing their duties on the mats.

"Blondie," purred General Gutsby, "me next." Her companion crawled off and I could see the face of the Guide who had met us at the bus.

"Me, too!" echoed Mr. Blossom. "Both of us. A double-header. I'm the bonus."

The General chuckled, the girl smiled. "It's friendship blendship!" said Blossom in a singsong manner.

"Service to mankind. Correct, dear?" the General asked, stroking the woman's hair.

"Service! You just love that word," Blossom observed. The General glared.

"Gutsie," chided Blossom, wriggling his rump in the General's face, "you've got to develop your sense of humor!" With a shriek of laughter he bounded away, pursued by the General who quickly caught him and wrestled him to the ground. Blossom gasped and tugged at the fingers around his neck. "Get away!" his choked voice spurted. "Maniac! It's my factory! Get off my property!"

"I run it, diddler," snarled the General. "YOU DO AS I SAY!" Each word took a short lift and crash of the head.

Blossom lay motionless. Was he dead? Serafina raised her head. I stood up. Why was I undisturbed by the violence, by our peculiar detachment, hardly more than idle curiosity?

Blossom was laughing. The General tickled him until he drew up his legs and turned over. Then the General threw himself on his friend.

I sat down, watching them, my compulsion swelling with smoke and sound and the heaving backside of General Gutsby, accepting a role in the scene. Formagraph coming to life.

The General disengaged himself. The two men returned to the Guide who reclined with her hands behind her head. Her firm breasts pointing deliciously upward. I glanced at Serafina's somewhat deflated bosom, pendulous and falling to one side as she leaned on her elbow. The young woman looked at me. I was drawn to her, instinct to instinct. Suspended in a process that soon would swallow me.

Serafina did not want to leave. "I feel good," she said dreamily. I watched her straining toward the trio beside us. The General crouched over the girl's head while Mr. Blossom straddled her legs. I had to reach Serafina, save myself. It was hard to move, hard to think. I swore and tugged her shoulders. She sat up shocked, beginning to cry.

We stepped through the maze of bodies. My head was throbbing with the ceaseless drum. And then a clear, lovely voice like a beam of light sounded through the haze. A tall, beautiful woman stood on a small, box-like platform, languidly swinging her naked body as she sang:

I've got freedom,
Freedom to love you.
I've got freedom,
Freedom to love you.
I've got freedom to l-o-o-o-ve you!

After each "love" she did a grind and bump until the last one, which she emphasized with a triple grind and bump. I recognized the tune—we occasionally heard it in the cafeteria. Groggy, feet dragging, something in me ran, ran, pulling my weighted legs and the reluctant woman at my side.

Freedom to love you,
The only freedom that counts.
Freedom to love you,
The only freedom that mounts.
I've got freedom to l-o-o-o-ve you!"

The voice stopped. A man hugged the singer. A woman clung to him. He shook off his admirer, catching her off balance so that she fell with an angry shout. She crawled back quickly and, grabbing the man's leg, bit it. He screamed and kicked her in the face.

A Guard clubbed the man to the ground, striking again and again at the unresisting figure whose features were blurring with blood. People nearby picked themselves up to stare at the fallen man, his cries collapsing into animal groans. Another Guard rushed over and pulled the victim to his feet. One could have fled the Camp unnoticed.

General Gutsby shouted at the bleeding head, "Damn you, this is a peaceful place! No room for fucking troublemakers!" He turned to the first Guard. "File a report, now!"

"Yes, sir!"

"This one's for the Game Room."

"No—please!" the man pleaded, suddenly alert.

"We need new security measures," said Blossom. "We can't have our workers damaged."

"Please! Please!—Oh God!"

"Spit that Godshit out of your mouth," snapped the General. "Security is my department," he growled at Blossom. "Don't sweat. His balls aren't damaged."

"His balls don't run the assembly line."

"Want to bet?" The General turned back to the first Guard. "File a report!"

"Immediately, sir," he saluted.

"The kind of fellow this country needs. A rock!" added Gutsby, slapping the Guard's bottom.

"Thank you, sir."

"Bring your report to me tomorrow morning—at 0900."

"Yes, sir!"

We didn't wait to learn the battered man's fate. I steered Serafina to the exit and opened the door that activated the cleansing shower through which we passed. Warm water, followed by sobering needles of ice. We endured the frigid spray until it stopped automatically and the door slid back. In the next room the bodydryer blew jets of hot disinfectant-smelling air all over us and somewhat cleared our heads. We were alert by the time we took our fresh gray uniforms. We put on the mocks and slippers and pressed the outdoor light button.

As we stepped out a tall, dark-haired Guide checked our wrist numbers and consulted a notepad. Serafina looked depressed. We had nothing to say. My room was closer so the Guide led us there first. On his cot, between the desk and the Candy Ma, Till lay snoring. The Guide let me into the empty room with a passkey. I glanced back at my wife, wondering if she had detected my relief.

S.

I lay on my cot, wanting to die. Tears could not wash away Poppa's accusing look. What had I done except follow his lead? It wasn't my fault or even his. My head continued to clear. I recalled the sweetish haze in the Love Room. Where was love in that wild place? I would never go back. Never! Not even to meet Poppa. That was how I felt.

When Dozie came in I pretended to be asleep. I wanted no comfort, deserved none. Wanted no one to touch me. Dozie called my name softly. I did not move. While he climbed into his bunk I lay wishing to crawl under the mattress and suffocate.

I cried again, a store of unshed tears that spilled over the room from every corner of my grief—my mother's death, my absent sons, the Service Camp, humiliation with Joseph, my whole life. Suddenly Dozie was beside me in bed, holding me like a child. It was a dream, a healing dream with a kindly man. I embraced it and kept my eyes closed. The man stroked my body patiently, firmly, with long strokes. He held me until I stopped crying, and we held each other in that sweet gentle dream until morning.

J.

I slept fitfully. A sense of loss encased me like a trash bag. Serafina's name: a moan in my chest, a breath I could not take. Her pale, wounded image brought tears to my eyes. How fragile she was. How self-righteous I was. I would pray to anyone now—. Help us, O GMI! Abandon hope, abandon hope, came the answer. GMI was a god like any other, pitiless, indifferent. Absent like God in that old priest's vacant church. We would die in the Service Camp one way or another. Escape. How? And if we failed?

Tears filled my heart for my lost family. Its dismantled life had been built with real love, as remote from the Love Room as I was from the past. Moira switched on the light and called up from her bunk, "Something bugging you? A lotta tossin' 'n turnin' upstairs."

"Nothing. Go to sleep."

"Had a good time last night?"

"Go to sleep. Yes."

"Told you so! Stuck with the ball and chain?"

"I'm tired. Good night."

"Couldn't get away, huh?"

"I didn't try."

"Too bad. Dozie and I had a lot of laughs, switching around. I think me being with you gives him a kinky thrill. He was hot stuff. Surprised the both of us. It's weird that Room but fun. You can let your hair down, really get down, know what I mean? Gives you a feeling of—" she searched for the word, "freedom."

"My God."

"What's the gripe now? You got to be philosophical. Okay, so it's tight quarters in here, but you get used to it. Have a positive attitude. Make believe this here's a motel. That itch you a little? It's a vacation, almost—no pots or pans, no washing the floors. Everything clean—like a hospital. They take care of you like a hospital.

"I was in one for a curettage and I wanted to stay a year. Nobody asking me 'What's for dinner?' The food was lousy I admit. It's better here. And the nurses got you up to get with the program, y'know?—like here, but I don't mind feeling I'm a kid for a change and my mother's taking care of me. A good mother, I mean, the kind you read about. Somebody making you chocolate pudding and cookies and buying you things. Ever have that? Mine was a witch, and I was washing her dishes and floors so she wouldn't chip her nail polish. My Pop was okay, but he drank and she threw him out. Then she threw me out when I wouldn't give her all my pay.

"I was on my own a long time before I met Dozie. I do kind of run things, I guess, but I'm tired of making dopey decisions—what to wear, what to cook, where to work, what TV to watch, what to do every goddamn minute. In a way we've got the cream, buddyboy. And I always say, when you've got the cream, pour the coffee." I reflected on this cryptic statement.

"Besides," she went on, "you can't win. So take it as it comes, or lays, or whatever the hell it does." She chuckled. "You'll live longer."

How could I confide in Moira the Unrestrained? And she already thought I was a strange one. She had kindness but lacked conviction. Moreover, she liked me. If I told her I wanted to escape, she would be miffed and fearful of blame. Enough motivation to turn me in. I wanted to discuss the matter with Serafina. Was I newly aware of her? Had I encouraged her enough to think for herself? Maybe she always did and I wasn't listening.

"I'll go back to the Love Room next Saturday."

"See!" Moira exulted, bounding out of bed. "I told you." She reached up and grabbed my thigh under the sheet. "You're loosening up, buddy-boy. We'll have a good time here too. You'll see."

The alarm sounded. Time for the Sector to rise, toilet, wash, dress, breakfast, toilet, exercise in the Gym, toilet, shower, lunch, toilet, watch TV, wait for dinner, toilet, eat, watch TV, toilet, sleep. A typical Sunday in the Camp.

Dear Mother and Father:

I have a shiny pin with three blue stripes. You should see it. The stripes mean 17 enemies. We have a smart Captain. He tells everybody I'm a good soldier. He teaches us to follow orders. It's for our own good. That's all for now.

Hail to our country.

Michael

I looked at the envelope with the censor-stamped corner. I reread the thin sheet of paper, searching for you, my son. I could not find you in the terse words or even between the lines. Had someone else written in your handwriting? Was a clone inhabiting you?

In my mind I fixed your image, trying to make it smile. You never smiled easily. Did you still love me? Had you ever? Me, timid, suspicious of the new order, of change, unwilling to oppose or completely to accept it? A querulous sort of person of small consequence, your father. Did you—do you judge him with pity, with contempt?

S.

The next morning I awoke in Dozie's muscular arms. There was no mock between us. What had I done? He saw the fear in my face, touched my lips softly with his. For a moment I felt protected. Then I pulled away. He looked so sad. When he rose I felt grateful and ungrateful. Ashamed. All my constancy—destroyed.

"Here is a letter for you," he said picking it up at the door. He stood naked. Only the letter mattered. Dozie put on his mock while I read.

Dear Momma and Poppa,

I know how to shoot a real rifle. It is very loud. I miss Momma's chicken and dumplings. We may write 50 words once a month. Please remember your promise. I have a friend. His cot is near mine. You promised. Hope to see you. PLEASE WRITE.

Your loving son,
Charles

Write! He had not received our meager letters! And now they would cease entirely. After the cold one from Michael and the wretched one from Charles, I wondered if our correspondence was a form of torture. I had written to my children, to you my dear ones. Little pleasure in sending short notes like bulletins but they were our tiny pitiful connection with you. Where did our words go Poppa's and mine? In almost four months only one letter from Charles and two from Michael. We could not even keep with us the few family photos we had brought. At home we had pictures on the piano. Instead they were held with our other belongings. I no longer expected to see any of those things again. I tried to sketch tiny pictures of you on the backs of your letters to recall your dear faces. The letters were collected and probably destroyed for "sanitary reasons." So much terror of microbes. Then I drew your faces on bits of toilet paper and managed to hide them under my mattress. I was learning to be sly.

"Remember your promise." Charles was ill! Through Dozie I communicated my panic to Joseph. An odd relay. Joseph seemed to agree with me. I imagined the boy feverish, maybe in a hospital. If only I could make him chicken soup. Strengthen it with my very bones. We had to find you, Charles. I heard you in my head all day no matter how many mysterious vials I handled. At night you troubled my dreams. Sometimes your face disappeared into monsters jumping out of gigantic pictures. I would wake up with a shout. Dozie came down from his bunk to comfort me.

The assembly line was getting weird. I was helping to arm missiles with something weird that went into the nose cones. Operation Open Arms they called it. Somebody had a devilish sense of humor.

I began to think harder about everything. Why did we dispose of our entire outfits daily—from hairnets to slippers? We were now fumigated before we showered. And why did some of the vials look different with things that floated and swam around in them? Things that we heard were changing on the slides and growing larger? Part of me was afraid to know.

J.

Moira had taken a sleeping pill. I'm not sure how she got one. When she began to snore, I took my hoard of Allowance Cards from my bunk, slipped them into my pocket, and descended quietly. Kneeling, I wiggled the envelope back and forth under the door to get Till's attention. The door opened. "What's up?" he announced grumpily.

"I must talk to you," I whispered. He let me out. The door closed behind me. We walked to his desk.

"Well?"

"It's about my son. I believe—that is I feel he may be sick."

"What did he say?" Till looked stern.

"Nothing. He didn't write anything."

"You have a sick feeling about nothing. Sounds as if you need the Doctor."

I had heard about seeing the Doctor. People returned from visits to the Nurse, but not always from the Doctor.

"I'm fine. It's just that my son—"

"Did he complain?"

"Oh, no! It was just the tone. He asks for us when he doesn't feel well. I know he wants to see us."

"Us?"

"My wife and me."

"His Mommy and Daddy," Till cooed.

"I'd like permission to visit him."

The Captain laughed. "You're a scream. First you want a change because your room isn't just right. Next you nearly start a riot in the cafeteria. Then you hassle General Gutsby and make more trouble for me. And now you want a leave of absence after a couple of months. Beautiful! You're at the front line whining for a leave of absence."

"Front line?"

"They didn't choose you for brains, did they. The peacekeeping work of the Service Camps makes them the front line. Same as the troops. Get it?"

"Are we at war?"

He looked at me pityingly. "There's always a war someplace, dummer. Don't you know anything? Anyway, once you're here, you're here."

"It's a five-year period," I reminded.

"Uh-huh."

"Five years according to the law."

"So maybe they extend it for emergencies. Maybe they make it up as they go along, who knows? They give the orders. It's their business."

"An emergency could go on and on . . ."

"Quit wasting my time! You got a good deal here. Whatsa matter, you constipated? You're talking crap. You'll be out of a job at this rate, Camper."

I ignored his threat. "Is there any chance of getting permission—for a couple of days? A day's pass?"

Till snickered. "A day trip. Like a casino bus? Who writes your material? No pass. Not even if you kiss my ass!" He laughed wildly. "Besides, there's no form." "Perhaps," I ventured, "I have something to offer you."

He glared. "What the devil can you offer me?"

I gulped. "My Allowance Cards. I've been saving them."

"Ha."

"The Soda as well as the Candy Cards."

"Big deal."

"And my Cigarette Card."

"What else?"

I had nothing more to give him. I took the offensive.

"We'll need our clothes. Just what we arrived in."

"Is that all?" he sneered.

"Yes."

"Good. Forget it."

"Any clothes will do. And shoes."

"Going bye-bye? You're a real nut job." He paused. "Besides, there are payoffs down the line. You don't have any other goodies, right? And if you're thinking of sneaking out, don't."

"How could I?"

"Yeah, you and your wife just want to play dress up. Better not try anything, or you'll end up in the Game Room."

I recalled the General's reference.

"You get Privilege of the Game Room after nine months. Target practice," he smirked, "with live targets. Show biz. Living theater, you know? I like the fat dames, huffing and puffing with boobs flying. Old guys racing around. It's a scream."

"God."

"You a religious freak too? Too many Gods in your mouth. Better spit 'em out."

"I need the clothes. I have money in the bank!"

"Sure, write me a check," he snapped. "Nobody can touch that, dumbbell, except the Government. Vathead! What good would money do me here?"

"For when you get out."

"Who knows. Who cares. I'm not bellyaching."

I was desperate. "At home I have two gold pieces, very old. They were in my father's family for generations—practically a family crest."

"A family who? Oh, you're a frigging lord now. Gold pieces—what am I supposed to do, stick 'em up my ass?" He removed his tinted glasses and rubbed his head. His eyes looked like steel.

"Say, there is something. Something special, you might say. How about a finger."

"What?"

"A little one you don't need for work. You could give me your pinky."

"That's crazy!"

"I'd rather have an eyeball. I'm kind of a scientist too, you know, on the side. It's a hobby. Starting a little collection in formaldehyde. I've got an eyeball. Might let you see it sometime. Nice to have a pair. A guy freaked out and took out his eyeball. Said it offended him, would you believe it?" Till chuckled. "That's the one I have. A souvenir."

"What happened to him?"

"Nosy little bastard aren't you. They couldn't do much with him. Bad news here and a rotten ad for us Upside. They sent him to the Game Room. Even with one eye he was pretty good at ducking the baseballs. A real comedy. Then they did stones. He lasted about an hour. What a mess on the floor." Till smirked. "Recycled him fast."

Uncertain whether Till was serious, I said, "I can't give you—that."

"What else you got? You're damn lucky I'm pissed enough about my promotion not to turn you in. Here I am, all set to go to the Tower and serve the General. A career move big time. Then they pass me over for a smartass bitchy blonde. I'm not complaining," he added quickly, "but fair is fair."

"My wife and I must get out of here. Our son is ill. It may be a matter of life and death!"

"You're crazier than Eyeball."

"Will you help us?"

"I ought to report you. You're headed for the Game Room. Or the Yard. Know about the Yard?"

"I'm not sure."

"An extra treat for Nine Month Workers. The Game Room's good for target practice. You need the activity. Tones you up. In the Yard you get your kicks watching all kinds of criminals: men, women, kids. Mostly from Upside. The variety's nice—fast, slow. When the D.F.S. does it you get a charge hearing that bang! But it's too quick." He shook his head.

"Hanging's better. You can get off on hanging. At least a hard on. Then take in the Game Room too like a double feature. Work out later in the Love Room. Mmmm." He put three fingers to his lips and blew a kiss.

My stomach churned. "Every week?"

"You gotta have stuff to look forward to, like the Love Room. The Yard is jumping most days, believe me, but only Saturday is public. You get that Privilege soon. The Game Room's a tasty Saturday special. Doesn't come easy. Like I said, you earn that after nine months."

"Suppose—there is no one to kill?"

"You kidding? Where you been living, in a Cradle? They always get somebody, even if it has to be one of us." He laughed. "Gotta have some fun."

"There's the Love Room," I said.

"Like that's enough."

"Suppose a Worker doesn't want to participate."

"It's a Privilege, damn it! They don't have to, but they do. We don't keep weirdoes here. Anyway, after nine months you'll be aching to kill anything. It keeps the bowels open, get me? We do everything here on a regular basis." He chuckled then added, "Gotta have order. No fuckups."

How could I have expected to move him for whom life and death had become a game? Captain Till was a product of the Service Camp, immune to suffering, love, my antique morality. Turning to leave I mumbled, "This was all a mistake. I—I haven't been sleeping well."

"Not so fast." His hand gripped my shoulder. "If you want to blow that bad—"

His reversal alarmed me. "I don't want to make trouble."

"Oh, ho! Daddy's getting cold tootsies."

"No, but—"

"Listen, Camper," he went on in a furious whisper. "I have a score to settle. That little bitch I mentioned. The one who brought you here from the bus—you've seen her. She was screwing around with the General and Mr. Blossom last Saturday night."

"I know the one."

"They promoted her! Sure, after she did both of them. How the fuck can I compete with that? Next Saturday will be her last Guide Duty for the Love Room. Bragged to me, the turd! She's going to General Gutsby in the Tower—the job I was scheduled for. She louses up my promotion and now I'm not good enough to trim her toenails."

"Your clothes are gone. Delete. This isn't a fucking warehouse, you know. But I *can* tell you a way out and get her blamed."

"We'd be recognized as Campers in these mocks." I was going along with the fantasy.

"Late at night, with nobody around, you'd have a chance to get home Upside. It's autumn. You won't be too cold. And you'll be running, probably," he added with satisfaction.

Autumn. To feel the sun again. To see the moon. Had leaves turned color? Were they still clinging to the trees? To walk in the park again with you, Charles, and with Momma, hear birds, children, return to the pond with our pebbles in it, bathe my lungs, my whole body in fresh air. The only children we might see here would be in the Game Room. Or the Yard.

"Take it or leave it," Till snapped. "You won't be back, no way. That's clear. So what do you say?"

On the run. Finding Charles and whisking him away somehow. Leaving Michael behind, perhaps forever. With his kills.

"Won't we need a document to visit the Home?" I was trying to think the matter through. "Yeah. Maybe I can get one, maybe not. Now the Cards."

My second thoughts took over. "Saturday."

"The Candy Cards then. Good faith, as they say. The rest on Saturday."

I surrendered them and he became businesslike. "Here's what you do. Saturday, go to the Love Room. When you and your wife leave the shower, after you dry off and get a clean outfit, the Guide opens the door. You step out, and she's supposed to take you to your Sector. The routine. But this time, you make her come inside."

"How?"

"Fake something. Pretend you're sick. Who cares? Anyway, get her inside."

"Then what?"

"Kill her." He was serious.

"I can't!"

He shrugged. "That's my plan."

"I can't kill in cold blood. I don't even know her."

"Figure it's a job. A contract."

"I don't have a weapon."

"Strangle her."

"Why?"

"You need time to get away."

"I could just knock her out, I think. I'm not terribly strong."

"She's not either. No self-defense training. Always goofing off and expecting Guards—especially me—to help her out. Phony bitch. Always sucking at the General. She never earned the job she has. Now she'll pay." He quivered with retribution.

"If we're caught, the charges would be less serious. Assault—not murder."

"Are you for real? Everything here's a capital crime. Saves time and jail space." His tone altered. "Maybe we ought to skip it. I don't want any bunglers bungling. If you fuck up, Camper, you'll be dead meat."

"I'll risk it, Captain."

"Well I won't risk it, dummy. I'm sticking my dick out. If things go wrong, I'll be in for it."

"I'm sure the Guide will be punished—severely—for letting us escape. They might even put her in the Game Room," I suggested cravenly, "and you would get her job."

"I'd like to see her in the Yard."

"If I do it," I continued, "there would be an investigation. The matter could get complicated for you—"

"Hold on, crapper, you threatening me?"

"No!"

"You're scared shitless. What are they letting into this place lately? You'll be sorry if she lives, I promise. And don't even think about vatting me. Bribers get offed quicker than anybody. You're already down as a troublemaker and a nut job." He stared at me. "Okay, suit yourself."

Suit? More of a bodybag. "What do we do next?"

"Go straight to the tunnel and walk through."

"Won't anyone be there?"

"Not weekends. They're cutting back. Talking about having no tunnel Guards at all. False economy, I say."

"How long is the tunnel?"

"Over a mile."

"Oh."

"A little hike."

"And then?"

"You'll be at the stairs on the left of the platform. Go up until you come to a metal door. Press the button on the right—got that?—the right side. The door will open and you take the lift to the street."

"Won't the exit be guarded?"

"There's a sentinel who walks up and down. Peek through the street door and leave the minute his back is turned."

"The door might be locked."

"Press the button on the right, like you did with the other door. It will slide open."

"Are you sure?"

"Positive. I saw it myself."

"You saw it?"

"Yeah. Well that's that. Let's get you back."

"Saturday," I repeated. "Saturday."

Lying on my bunk afterward, it became clear. Till was an ambitious scoundrel who would use Serafina and me to advance himself. He might even arrest me — us. My wrist itched. I scratched the scabs till they started to bleed.

Nauseated, I felt the sweat trickling down my armpits. Should I retract everything as a bad joke and offer the surrendered Candy Cards as my apology? I would smile, clap Till on the shoulder, my hand lingering sincerely. If necessary I would kneel (as I had to General Gutsby and Mr. Blossom), extend all my Allowance Cards, grateful to have them snatched before I was dragged away on my hands and knees.

Tears dropped like spittle on my face, as if the very walls were showering their disgust. Surely I deserved to be as miserable as I was. Courage to act demanded courage to be wrong. Anxiety and indecision were killing me anyway. There was less to lose than I had supposed. Serafina and I were now committed to action. Irrevocable spoken words. Till would retaliate if I reneged. I scratched my wrist raw.

My mind was the troublemaker. Moira was right. Make the best of what you couldn't control. Better still, enjoy it. Wasn't the work easy, with two women and a regular schedule of diverting rewards? Loathsome. The Service Camp had replaced my family with a few unsatisfactory letters and the Love Room.

I was adapting to Moira, the Camp, my deadly work. Soon Serafina and I might grow to enjoy the Love Room, welcome its release. Moira did. Then one day we would stop making appointments with each other and merely go there. The State would swallow us, regurgitate our love.

That fateful morning Serafina and I had stood together in line, she right behind me. How frightened she was. I only wanted to show her it was all right. I had bungled. It was my fault. Yet why had an organization seemingly precise in detail left our housing to chance? To places in a line? I thought of the mysterious Game Room. The Yard. Till's collection in formaldehyde. Cruelty permeated the Camp, seeping into every level. No need for the State to assert its power over me. I had already capitulated, forfeited my family.

Family. I remembered Gutsby's contempt — that's what it was. Obtrusive in the new order? "Downsize the plants," Blossom had joked. Was it a joke? And the growing unemployment and unrest—we could see what was happening in our own lives. As for the Government, the arms and security programs that finally sank it in debt—were we the ultimate solution? Slave labor of dependable, healthy citizens—the National Honor List? Sex pacified us and stimulated production. It sold the product: the State itself.

S.

While Joseph seemed preoccupied, Dozie was growing more considerate. The man could not help being coarse. It was like carrying a wart on his nose. For the first time I tried to imagine myself married to someone else. Dozie said I was the first person who ever listened to him. Even I could recognize exaggeration but his remark flattered me. Maybe he was complaining about his wife. How could she hear him when she was so loud and garrulous? I was used to listening to people. Dozie asked me about my life and my children. I liked to talk to him. Not that Joseph wouldn't listen to me though his father was a different matter. How he hated it when I grew bolder and voiced my opinions. "Where is the nice girl my son married?" he used to ask after Michael was born as if I'd hid her under the table or stuffed her into a pillowcase. I wasn't a girl either. I was a woman. Dozie reminded me of that all the time.

There was a tender side to the man, appealing in a specimen of his size and strength. Specimen—the word conjured up the vials. Why were some of them changing color? Did particles move around in them or was it my eyesight? Was I getting used to more weird things in my daily life?

Dozie. On the assembly line sometimes I thought of him. I guess as a kind of escape. No, as a person. He never had a real chance to be educated. To develop talents he might possess. He had to leave school and get a job when his father couldn't support the family. His role was set a little the way mine was. Now that was a funny thought and what harm could thoughts do? Dozie looked up to me and liked my talk. It was not like being with Poppa who was so smart I would mostly just listen. Again and again the image of Charles lying ill in the Home made me tremble and I feared making some terrible mistake dropping or throwing vials or shouting and running up and down the aisles. Joseph must do something. I could only nag.

J.

What a fool I had been with Till! If Serafina and I tried to escape and were caught, we would never see Charles or Michael or anyone else ever again. Finished. And if we succeeded, where would we hide? In our house? In the basement or the attic? Too dangerous. We would have to find Charles quickly, reassure him, then leave town without him. He would cry but we couldn't take him with us. We'd live on the run. Crazy. Should we try to withdraw money from the bank? Too risky. We did have the gold pieces, quite valuable these days. We would need money, traveling far, being hunted down. Ending up as targets in the Game Room. Or the Yard. I ached with conflict. My hand swelled.

Perhaps Charles was healthy. We might just be getting him into trouble. At the Home they knew we were supposed to be in the Camp. We were all on that damn List! We would have no Form to present—Till would not even bother trying. We'd need a bogus one or a way to see Charles in secret. And if he insisted on going with us? What a harebrained scheme! I was demented. I resolved to do nothing.

In a dream I saw you, Charles, floating somewhere above the horizon. I rose from my bunk right through the ceiling into the sky where you were waiting. I looked down in horror: the lower half of my body was gone. I tried to descend and retrieve it when Captain Till appeared, holding the rest of me under his arm like the bottom half of a mannequin, literally a dummy, as Till had called me. He threatened to keep his trophy unless I went through with the escape. He held my legs by the ankles and waved the naked fragment, taunting me. You receded. I grew weaker and weaker. Arteries and veins hung from my insides and my heart fell out. I was hollowing out, crumbling. In the last image Till held my healthy half by the penis and waved my loins triumphantly over his head while my upper half whirled away like dry leaves on the wind.

I felt a familiar sensation under the sheet. Moira was giving me her manual greeting. I turned over quickly and looked down.

"Hi, buddy. Having wet dreams?"

"Leave me alone."

"You were moaning and groaning. Boy, you sleep like a dead herring. Didn't you hear the alarm? What a goddamn racket just to get us up in the morning. They oughta have music. A dance band. What you need is an eye opener."

I pushed her hand away and climbed down. "You look gloomy, kid." She put her arms around my neck.

"Moira, I'm serious. Do you think people are content here?"

"Why not?"

I gently removed her hands and stepped back. "Don't they complain?"

"You oughta get your cafeteria seat changed. Sittin' next to the Captain you gotta play statue. Talk to anybody on the job?"

"No."

"That's smart, I guess, after the ruckus you've made. Look, you can tell me anything 'cause I like you. And you gotta admit I'm broad-minded. But one of these days somebody's gonna think you're an instigator or something. A leftover Terrorist. Don't forget we have an audience," she whispered. "That could mean trouble, honey, and I'm not buying any. You could land in the Game Room. Worse."

"You know about the Game Room?"

"Where you been? And the Yard. Cafeteria stuff. But you're always moping or looking to see your wife. Okay," she softened, "sitting by Lover-boy Till gives your end of the table a bum leg." She laughed.

"I wonder if people like the Game Room. And the Yard."

"Nobody in our Sector's been here long enough, at least not for the Game Room, but sure. Why not? It's a Privilege. Not easy to come by, you know. Takes nine whole months." She was instructing a dull pupil.

"A gestation period."

"What?"

"A monster," I mumbled. "You believe throwing stones at people is an honor?"

"BB guns too sometimes. We're talking criminals here. They oughta do something useful on their way out. Look, Government says it's an honor so it's an honor."

"And if they say it's a punishment—"

"What are you talking? Cut it out. You're messing me up with this crap."

The door opened and we lined up for the toilet. As I passed Captain Till, he tapped me on the shoulder.

"Saturday," he whispered.

Our conversation could not be wished away. Fearful, I prepared to explain my change of heart.

All day I worried. What had I done? The plan was absurd. Instead I had created a new problem: Till.

He was intelligent. He would be reasonable. I would point out the perils more clearly, careful to avoid insulting his scheme. As for his unusual hobby—the eyeballs, etc.—well, nobody's perfect.

Behind the pinprick pupils of my work supervisor's eyes lurked accusations. My shoulder tensed as he peered over it noting my computations. The slide creatures seemed more numerous and lively than ever. It was harder to count them. Their odd shapes grew larger.

At meals I kept my counsel as usual, seated near or beside Captain Till, who insisted on my proximity ever since my cafeteria outburst. I could produce little in the way of acceptable chitchat. What could I say to him—how can you stand this place? Where is Form 1040ZZ? I managed little beyond "Please pass the salt." A gift, this ability to chatter. We didn't even have weather to talk about, yet talk flowed in a constant murmur: sex, work, war, TV, the Love Room. We were now permitted to speak softly, though some still conversed in whispers.

I stared at the far end of the cafeteria where Serafina was eating. Dozie said something to her and she laughed. If she looked my way she didn't try to catch my eye. After dinner we marched back to our Sector. Till stood by the lavatory door, stuffing candy into his mouth. We washed up, filed out, and were let into our rooms. At my doorway I pretended to stub my toe.

"What happened?" Moira called.

"Nothing. I'll be there in a minute." I pulled the door shut and faced the Captain. We were alone.

"Well?" he asked.

"I can't do it." The words were out, but the arguments were stuck inside.

"Oh?"

"I can't."

"You'd better."

"I'll give you all the Allowance cards. All of them."

"Listen, Camper, nobody craps out on me, okay? Saturday." He emphasized the date with a push into the room.

"What was that about?" asked Moira.

"I stubbed my toe."

"Weren't you talking to him?"

I desperately wanted to confide in her. I would have spoken to a cockroach, but without jeopardizing Serafina and myself any further. "I once told him I wanted to get out."

"You *are* crazy. I don't want to hear about it."

"It was a joke."

"Don't you like me?"

"What does that have to do with anything? I told you it was a mistake. I thought my son might be ill."

"Is he better?"

"How should I know? He probably was just homesick."

"So you had to cut out. Crawl away when my back was turned. Am I such a dog? I thought we were getting along peachy. Just goes to show."

"Please don't take it personally."

"I got the signals, all right, but I'm a dope for hope. It was so convenient and all. I'll put in for 1040ZZ myself or whatever the hell it is. Yeah, I'll ask for a room change."

Her agitation meant trouble. "They could reunite you with Dozie."

"Not him, the louse! He's happy with your ex—I mean your wife, or didn't you notice. I don't give a damn what he does. So there won't be a switch with wifey or anything like that, before you get your hopes up." I tried to ignore her remark about Dozie and Serafina.

"What reason would you give?"

"Who knows? Maybe I'll say I don't want to be locked up with a troublemaker who wants to scram."

"Please don't."

She narrowed her eyes. "I'll have to think it over."

"Moira," I implored, "you are a first-rate companion. First-rate. Believe me."

"Like shit."

"I swear!"

"You got a funny way of showing it. Make me feel I'm a pest. I'm not used to chasing guys. You oughta see me at a bar. In five minutes they're bunchin' around like bees."

"I can imagine."

"I don't need your insults."

"I didn't mean—"

"Treats me like I have the clap," she told the sink.

"I assure you—" In a surge of terror I threw my arms around her. "You are a very satisfactory roommate."

"Now he tells me," she announced to the wall. A woman scorned. A hungry crocodile.

"It's the truth." I smoothed her hair. It sprang back accusingly.

"Prove it." She stared at me.

I smiled faintly, wishing she might see us with a touch of humor.

"Now." She had turned malicious.

Moira was pushing me too far. I could feel the crunch of crocodile jaws.

"O-o-o-o!" I dropped my hands and clutched my chest.

"What's the matter?"

"It's nothing—my heart—it will pass. Just let me sit in the chair." I eased myself down.

"You have a bum heart?" Moira asked incredulously.

"No—I don't think so. It may be indigestion."

"Maybe I give you gas."

"A little water, please."

She handed me a cup. I took a sip.

"That's better." I managed a brave smile.

"Funny how it came on," she mused. "Then again, a friend of mine ate fried chicken for dinner and dropped dead over the apple pie, right after he asked for a scoop of vanilla. You had a physical though, when we came here."

"I said it's probably indigestion. Plus stress. A side order," I joked, wanly attempting to mimic her style.

"You ought to see a doctor. I'll call Till."

"Please!" I grabbed her arm and would have bitten it. "Don't bother."

"Next time you might konk out," she said coldly.

"It won't happen. I'm certain. I only need rest."

"You mean no sex." She was ruthless.

"I'll feel better tomorrow."

I climbed into my bunk and glanced down at her. She gazed at me skeptically. I recalled sea monsters guarding a passage in that old story by a deaf poet—or was he blind? Whatever, I had to navigate between danger and disaster, one here, the other outside. To whom could I turn?

My father is sitting in the maroon armchair, his large, slippered feet propped on a footstool, his back to the window. In the pale light of a winter afternoon he is reading a book. He must have read it before, from that small store we kept. I stand behind him, pressing my nose against the cold pane. Three boys play in the falling snow.

"May I go out, Father?"

He turns, sees the boys running about, laughing and throwing snowballs.

"It's snowing," he replies. "Finish your homework."

"I finished it."

He scowls. "Go help your mother."

His command is final. First, my mother already showed signs of the frailty that began after my brother left home, that would claim her after he was killed. Second, the man was my father. Or first and second too because he was my father. My mother sits at the kitchen table, shelling peas.

"Father says to help you."

"There's nothing to do." Her smile, sweetly brave, is rarely joyful. "I want to play outside. He thinks you need me."

She understands. Sighing because she wants to support me without contradicting him she says, "You can help me shell the peas." She knows I like to pop a few raw ones into my mouth like green pellets of candy. "Then you can check the silver to make sure it's dry." The newly polished knives and forks lay on a towel, ready to be replaced in a drawer. I sensed her complicity.

"He doesn't want me to play with the boys."

"He's afraid you'll get wet in the snow and catch cold."

"I want to play."

Her sad expression fills me with guilt. "Listen to your father," she says helplessly. I sit beside her, rewiping the spoons.

The cold of his command. Intimidating. Unshakable. It could bend one as my mother and I were bending over the table. Not until his final illness did I see him as a frightened man. At the end he was still imposing when I drew the warm soapy washcloth across his broad, wasted chest. A man from another country whose grandfather had been shot in front of his house and his grandmother disappeared, a man whose father had been exiled in war and became an itinerant tailor in our country after his wife abandoned him and the child. Brought up by Aunt, with whom they settled. By thirteen he was an orphan. He lived with Aunt while he went to school, worked at the chemical plant and attended college at night, worked hard all his life.

I think he liked chemicals because they had predictable properties and they wouldn't disappear. A handsome man, taller than my brother and me, an employed man at that, he had no trouble finding a wife: my mother. We had no pets except for goldfish now and then. He had once been bitten by a dog and disliked pets in general. I imagined him standing in the doorway of his beloved house, keeping the snarling world at bay.

My father had more excuses than I who slipped into his chair, my back to the window of existence. I too had ignored the family of strangers that could intrude at will.

S.

I could do nothing without Joseph and he was vacillating. My whole life I had depended on him. Feminism had come and gone and where was I, wife and mother with all my homemaking skills? Assembling death. Waiting for the "privilege" of seeing Poppa. Sharing publicly a moment that used to be private. That should be so. Now Poppa was a candy treat and Dozie was my friend. A crazy situation! We would never receive permission to visit Charles. We were in prison. We had to escape.

J.

Friday morning I lay sleepless, exhausted. Could I live like this, keeping Moira at bay, worrying about Serafina with Dozie? If Moira were to be my only dependable release, wouldn't I be using her as a sexual toilet? Till might be aiding our flight in order to gain more victims for the Game Room and the Yard. He might receive a commission. Was he really intent on promotion to the Tower and taking revenge on the Guide? Maybe Blondie was his collaborator. Had he lied about everything?

If we refused to go he'd be vengeful, have us arrested for conspiracy, bribery, almost any charge he chose. He already held my Candy Cards as evidence. Moira, sizzling with frustration, might support his allegations and add a few of her own. I guessed Serafina would want to go, never mind the consequences. Charles's health, Charles all the way. What about us? Could I change her mind? She seemed different, less pliable. Dozie's influence. What a wretched survival we faced. For five years. Maybe.

The Camp itself. The toxic roots of reality were here, showering Upside like a rain of deadly leaves mulching the earth. Love, Honor, Game, Yard. Were these distortions our country's own hybrids? What if Michael risked death and Charles suffered and Momma and I were cut apart for nothing. And there was something else. What was happening to those microbes? I felt profoundly uneasy. This was no retreat from the world. It was dangerous here.

S.

Praying that Joseph had arranged something, I pulled the sheet away from my face. Saturday morning. I felt restless, light-headed, as if the sweet haze of the Love Room were already reaching me. Poppa will be a magician, I thought. He will take us out of this place, save our poor family. Our sick child crying for his parents, a need that must be respected.

"I wish we had children," Dozie was saying sympathetically. "Moira couldn't. We talked about adopting. Kept talking about it, I did, anyway. Then we stopped. You know how things go.

"It's tough when your parents leave you the way Moira's did. Mother threw her out, imagine. What a rotten break. They say being on your own early makes you strong. Baloney. It wears you down. You push too much or you let people push you around."

Dozie was sensitive. He continued to surprise me. When I couldn't resist reaching out my hand he closed his over mine.

J.

I had done everything wrong plus presuming Serafina would agree. Saturday morning, on the way to the toilet I signaled to Till who ignored me. Breakfast-bound afterward, he poked me and whispered, "Don't get smart." So the matter was resolved. I endured the rest of the day until time for the Love Room.

Desire and dread squeezed my life between them. Guilt flooded me like a clogged latrine. Why did I involve you so casually, Serafina? Not casually—a fact of our lives, this being together. How else should I have handled the matter? Till would have implicated you for spite. But you had the right to decide for yourself. I was seeing you as a separate person, apart from my decisions and needs. Difficult when we had always been a unit. "Every pot has its cover," my mother used to say. Still, you deserved a choice, more so in view of my ambivalence. The idea seemed new.

We lined up outside the Love Room. The same phony orchids banked the doorway like purple labia. I concentrated on Serafina beside me, on her gentleness that would soon caress my face, dissolve the nightmare.

"We can leave tonight," I whispered, and hastily explained: Till, the bribe, Form 1040ZZ, the flight to Charles. I mentioned hazards, asked her to choose. She looked away. When we neared the door she replied softly, "Don't you want me with you?" I pressed her hand and quickly told her the plan, skipping the violence.

Inside, we deposited our mocks and again walked naked into the Love Room. The dim, reddish-blue light, sinuous with narcotic sweetness, fell in a haze on the writhing flesh. Each breath carried into my body the moans and laughter that surged through the drumbeat. I felt looser, weaker, my sensuality checked by a gnawing below my ribs. I concentrated on my possible ulcer, glad of the pain that eluded the force of the Room. We found a mat and lay there quietly. Wait too long, we might succumb to our bodies. Leave too soon, we would arouse suspicion.

Serafina was getting drowsy. "They will catch us."

My stomach pain increased. I could use it as an excuse if we were stopped. My hand itched. Serafina was right, but I was a bull that Till had prodded into the ring. No room in the stall to turn around. But Serafina could.

"You can stay. It's all right. Better for you." I tried to sound convincing.

She closed her eyes and I thought she was going to sleep. "I'll go with you." Her voice was toneless but her eyes opened. My heart leaped.

"Come on."

We zigzagged between the mats toward Exit and stepped into the shower. The water struck my skin with relentless logic. Till had duped me! Slight, quivering, Serafina stood beside me. I tried to appear resolute.

We dried ourselves and hurried into fresh gray uniforms. Having instructed my wife, I pressed the outdoor light button. The door opened. It was Blondie.

I pointed to Serafina, who sat in a corner with eyes closed. "Please come in. I think she's ill."

The Guide hesitated. When she stepped forward I shut the door. She wheeled in surprise and I caught her on the jaw with my fist. The blow infuriated her. She started and I clutched desperately at her throat. She hooked her fingers at my eyes.

"No, no!" murmured Serafina from the floor. I squeezed the pale throat tighter until the Guide released her grasp. She collapsed at my feet.

"You killed her!" Serafina whispered, horrified.

"She's breathing. Let's go!"

It was hard to keep from running. We followed the corridor outside the dormitory until we came to the long, open platform of the station. The tunnel lay ahead to the left. Nearby, separated into two lanes by a metal bar raised some two feet off the ground stood two buses like the ones that had brought us. I held Serafina's hand tightly, preparing to dash, when I saw a Guard carrying a rifle.

Till had not warned me.

The clicking bootsteps approached. We flattened ourselves on the ground. Nowhere to hide. We lay there rigid. Targets.

The steps paused, then receded. When the Guard strode halfway to the opposite wall, we bolted forward and leaped down into the bus path. We crossed the metal bar and huddled between the vehicles. My teeth chattered. Serafina held her scratched knee. Again the clicking approached.

The dark mouth of the tunnel was perhaps fifty feet ahead. As the Guard passed the cars I glimpsed his boots and signaled to Serafina.

Holding our slippers we ran, half-expecting a shout or a shot or even an electronic beam triggering floodlights or an alarm. We reached the tunnel.

Soon we could see nothing but darkness. Feeling the clammy wall with my right hand, I extended my left behind me to Serafina. In the silence I heard her rapid breathing at my shoulder. She tried to keep pace with my longer strides. I took her hand. The ground stretched flat and smooth, unmarred by tracks or ties to stumble over. We heard faint sounds ahead, like rustling leaves. As our eyes adapted to the dark we noticed small things scurrying ahead. Too small for rats. Mice? We put on our thin slippers.

A third car supposedly rested at the end of our path. Till had mentioned a total of three air-powered buses, those which had brought us to the Camp. One should be standing at the terminal ahead. The metal bar continued dividing the lanes.

Guiding ourselves by the wall, we proceeded in a direct path. As our eyes adjusted further we discerned the oval shape of the tunnel. There was light in the distance and we had barely traveled half a mile. Was there someone ahead?

I held Serafina's hand more tightly. We listened. The light neither brightened nor dimmed. We moved on until we could see a small, flat bulb in the ceiling. "Our star," I whispered. Perhaps the bulb concealed a surveillance camera or a listening device. Why was it there? Had the tunnel been left completely unguarded?

We hurried along, glad for the return of darkness, pausing only to rub our sore feet. The slippers were wearing out. And then there was an arc of light. We were coming to the end.

Till had assured me the station would be deserted. Serafina and I hugged each other, frozen. Remaining in the tunnel seemed almost an alternative.

"We have to keep going," I said. We crouched, inching forward. Gradually we could see the bulk of a vehicle—the third car—and the line of a platform on the left.

There was no sound or movement, no clue to safety or a trap. We had to act.

I stepped behind Serafina. The ground sloped gently toward the Service Camp. Along that incline I spilled my kidneys' puny defiance.

At once dozens of creatures of varying sizes scurried from the darkness to stud either side of the narrow stream. Hissing through multiple mouths, they sucked up the liquid. I clutched Serafina's shoulder. When she turned the creatures disappeared.

"You saw them?" I gasped.

She nodded.

"They remind me of something."

"The slides," she said. "The microbes."

"They're growing in the tunnel."

We wanted to run but had to creep along the divider, halting again and again, fearing to see a creature or a person who might be following us. I dreaded to hear anything yet was alert to every sound until we emerged from the tunnel and reached the car. We pressed our bodies against the cushioned base of the vehicle.

Still there was silence. I peered up at the platform. To the left I saw an open staircase. I remembered something about Jacob and the ladder of heaven.

"Now!"

We climbed over the rail and clambered onto the platform tearing our mocks. We ran up the steps that circled to a metal door. I found the button on the right. Beyond that door rose the lift to a second door and freedom. I hesitated, my finger poised over the little square. Till had clearly specified the location. There were two buttons, however. Both were unmarked. The one on the left confused me. I had to rely on information. I had to rely on Till.

I pressed the button on the right. An alarm sounded.

We ran. Back down the stairs, jumping stumbling hurtling our cumbersome bodies to the ground.

"Stop! Stop!" came a voice from above. Then shots. Our minds dropped to our feet as we dashed to the platform and leaped into the empty path. Serafina tripped over something—a creature? I took her hand as we sprinted back toward the blackness. A floodlight beamed from the station behind us.

Caught like moths, we threw ourselves on the ground. "I'm sorry," I kept repeating to Momma. She cried.

We clung to each other. No more doubt, hope, fear, no more conflict or flight or plans going awry, no more worry about bizarre creatures or armed humans. Wrenched apart by a Guard, roughly handcuffed, we were pushed toward the bus and rushed back to Camp. Momma's stricken face—that was what I took to my cell. I never saw her again.

S.

Joseph. I say your name. The sound of it keeps you with me. The creatures! I see them crawling up the wall—raining down on the Camp. Raining terror! They climb into the street where my poor Charles is weeping. Michael shoots at them. They multiply faster. Thousands run everywhere Upside and stream back down into the Camp. Hungry! They eat the Laboratory the Love Room the missiles uniforms Allowance Cards. They eat the General and Mr. Blossom. Till. Everyone. I make a list in my head. Everything eaten even the walls. At last I can see daylight.

One morning a Guard gives me a pen and paper. The Camp authorities want me to write a confession. They say they will let Michael and Charles read my account after I die. They will inherit my poor words. Soon? Will the authorities compare my story with Poppa's? I figure that the more I write the longer my survival. So I have been writing the story of my life. Maybe these words will reach my sons like an embrace from the grave. I struggle to do that.

The authorities want my notes. They keep the light on in my tiny cell. Nobody bothers questioning me. Guards keep reminding me I'll be executed. When? They get furious if I ask for you so I stop. I feel desperate to speak to someone. I could ask for Dozie, but don't. Why bring him trouble. Not that they'd grant any request of mine. I think of him kindly with longing for those peaceable days. Does he wonder about me? Does anyone except you, Joseph? I resign myself to isolation. I think of your father sitting in his chair near the window. A window! Will I ever see the sky? When I die I want to fly with seagulls. I'll be a spirit with wings.

I beg to see my children. Nobody seems to care that Michael is important, a member of the Distinguished Firing Squad. Or that Charles needs me. One visit please please somebody reading this. Guards are stone gods indifferent to suffering. Just write it down they say. Is this supposed to keep me from screaming and crying? It does. I thank my two friends, paper and pen. Especially paper to whom I keep talking. I kiss them both. I kiss special words—*Joseph, Charles, Michael*. I kiss those words. The Guards collect my pages. No reaction. My boring life—who wants to read about it? Or live it? I plod on with my scribblings.

My new cell has a view of the Yard. I glance at the prisoner standing against the wall. It is not Poppa. The wall and the ground are marked with blood. They wash some off but it stains the cement. I've learned to turn away quickly before the rifle shots and not look back. Sometimes they wheel a platform over and I hear the scaffold's trap door spring open. Saturday there is a crowd watching. I can hear the shouts and the roar. GMI! GMI! All the Yard sounds keep repeating and join the tunnel creatures crawling through my head.

Every few days somebody collects my scribblings without directly touching anything I've handled. The Guards begin to wear sanitary masks, white mocks and gloves, like outfits we wore on the assembly line. They spray me and the room every morning with a disinfectant. Must be afraid of contamination from the tunnel. I want to see the creatures grow bigger with more mouths, thicker lips, tongues long enough to suck in the whole Camp. I want to contaminate everything. The light stays on all night. I don't care. I'm writing all the time.

At times I feel angry with Poppa. It was a bad idea from the beginning. I should have said no. I should have used my own judgment. Anger and guilt make me very sad. We haven't even said goodbye.

J.

They throw me into a cell and interrogate me. No beating. I am surprised and grateful. The Guard tells me General Gutsby himself is coming. I say as little as possible. The General will question me tomorrow.

If I could sleep the cement bunk would make it impossible. For hours I sit reviewing events. Gullible, stupid, no insult is too harsh for me. Hard to bear this remorse.

General Gutsby rushes in. He is wearing a blue mock and rubber gloves. Impatiently he pulls the mask down from his face.

"Sit!" he commands. I sit on the bunk. He stares and shakes his head. "Your son Michael is a hero. He distinguishes himself in battle. And you—" The General coughs with rage.

"May I see him?"

"You are asking for a Privilege? Now? I doubt he'll want to see you."

"If I explain—"

"Explain!" the General splutters. "What's to explain? You have disgraced yourself, your family, the National Honor List, the Service Camp, your country, your Sector, the human race—you name it. Mr. Blossom and I work our balls off to keep this country from being blown to hell— have you no pride, Camper? No sense of decency? Since you apparently don't have any brains?" He pointed to his head. "Drafty up there, eh?

"You," shaking his finger at me, "you are the first, the very first lunatic to do what you have done. You're immoral. You're shit. Explain *that* to your son."

If I were not seated, his righteous fury could have knocked me down.

"I wanted to visit my boy."

"At his battlefront?" Gutsby is incredulous.

"My younger son, Charles—in the Young Patriots' Home. My idea," I emphasize. "My wife is innocent."

"Idiot! You know you have to apply through channels."

"I was told Form 1040ZZ did not exist."

"Subversive talk!"

"Captain Till said so."

"Stop ducking the blame. You're a coward. Anyway, there's Form 1040MM for miscellaneous requests."

"He said no one could leave."

"Correct."

"I'm supposed to fill out a useless form?"

"Not for you to say."

"Sir, excuse me, it makes no sense."

The General reddens. "I decide what makes sense! If everyone started asking dumb questions, we'd have anarchy. More Terrorists! What do you bet would happen to our democracy?"

"Democracy?"

"Imbecile! How did you ever qualify for the Service Camp? You and your wife enjoy special considerations because your son is a hero. He will be notified before you're both shot."

He pulls up his mask and turns to leave. He says through the mask, "By the way, did you see anything in the tunnel?"

"It was dark."

"Anything—out of the ordinary?"

"No."

"Anything that moved?"

"Like bugs?"

"Yes—anything."

"No."

He glares accusingly over his mask before moving on. I want to blurt out my information but hold back. I can tell he already knows something. And we have been condemned to death. What has Serafina told them? Let the whole Camp die. If escaped microbes are mutating and breeding in the tunnel, let them thrive. I would drink a glass of champagne to that. Raise one of my mother's crystal goblets in a toast. Let something escape! The creatures—they are what this frenzy is about. Gutsby is playing it down. Panic control. For the first time since our capture, I smile.

The next day a Guard brings me a loose-leaf notebook and a pen. They want my story, he says. They want to study me to locate flaws in the system. I am a celebrity. When I ask about my wife, he shrugs.

Maybe ours was not the first escape attempt. Were people so docile, accepting as "honor" this slavery unto death, this enslavement by death itself? There is progress in my thinking, do you agree, Reader of these lines?

Every few days the written pages are removed. I ignore the tunnel, write about the Camp. Review my early life. Might wallowing in contrition keep me alive? The authorities are marking time until Michael's arrival. Lucky to have a son in Military Service. He may save us yet. No one speaks to me anymore. I am writing my testament. So be it.

Through the small barred window I see a prisoner in the Yard. Can this woman be Serafina? No, my wife is at home preparing the house for our return, taking down white sheets from the pictures, uncovering chairs. She stands at the kitchen stove, cooking chicken and dumplings for the family.

Noisy with suffering the unruly dead enter my cell. They crowd me. Under the corpses I gasp for air. Tunnel creatures seethe and nibble their flesh, nibble mine. My body smells of rot. Disinfectant can't kill the odor.

I am turning to compost. Creatures grow out of my skin, larger and larger. Where is anybody's God? Serafina's? The God of the drunken priest? He wears boots like General Gutsby and walks arm in arm with him and Mr. Blossom. They march around the Yard. Or is God in the tunnel, biding his time. His wrath.

Michael, when you come here wearing your uniform and accomplishments, will anyone dare to harm us?

Serafina. A touch in the Love Room. A glance in the cafeteria. I long for those good old days.

Two boys stand on a platform, crying. What could they have done? The Saturday audience rumbles and whistles. What sport is this? The Distinguished Firing Squad marches in, one two, one two. And there you are my fine son, Michael, wearing a splendid green uniform. You hold a rifle. The boys cry. Another clerical error. When will they get anything right? In the row you aim your weapon. You are a rifle. Michael the Child Killer. Fire!

I demand to see you. Who is this Hero of the State who fills me with loathing and fear? My living stigma, my survivor, my heir. Better the tunnel creatures. Let them take over the Camp, the whole country. My lost future. My broken heart.

General Gutsby stands outside my cell. He wears a sanitary mask this time, and gloves. His uniform is again hidden under a disposable blue gown. His head looks red.

"Vomit!" he calls hoarsely through the bars, "You're vomit and shit! You said nothing about what you saw in the tunnel. We had to read it from your stupid notebook! You're filth! Contamination! I forbid you to say another word to anybody or to write another word about this. You're going to be exterminated like those vermin you think you saw. You want to spread havoc? Think we'll permit that? Let you vat our whole fucking system? You Enemy Terrorist!"

I will die in the Yard. Something more than a number. Enemy Terrorist. A person. To be cremated? Recycled? Will you be my executioner, Michael? Ease me down a dispo chute?

Under that uniform somewhere its fabric touches my shoulders. Child Killers. Your finger and mine pulling the trigger. Son and Father. Apple and tree. I cannot bear this guilt or understand it. I reject it. I think of Charles, Serafina, the falling snow. Let me sit in my father's chair, rest my feet on the hassock. So tired now. Forgive me, my son. I forgive you.

S.

Joseph. You march to the wall. No no. It is a nature path by the pond. Trees shrink into young men in green uniforms with rifles. I can't think them away. The tall one the beautiful one—I feel it in my skin growing cold—it's Michael. Last time too—was that my son who faced two boys on a platform? I couldn't look. I wept. Michael the Terrible. Poppa stands there in the same place. It can't be happening. Run—run down the nature path. Away from the Yard. Pebbles bleed into the pond. I scream and scream. Don't Michael! Please don't! Please look at the man—it's your father, it's Poppa! Executioner! This is Momma. Can you hear me? May you boil in your father's blood. May the creatures find you and gnaw off your murderous fingers and chew your eyes that aim death. May the Firing Squad come for me.

Epilogue

Dear Charles:

I regret to inform you Father is dead. Mother is in prison. Her fate will be decided. I have credits on my record so maybe that will help.

Shame is on the family. Our parents, mostly Father since he decides everything, they betrayed our country. They tried to run away from their Service Camp. Remember we were proud to serve? They changed.

As reward for kills at the front I was assigned to the DFS (Distinguished Firing Squad). Yesterday Father was brought out and a few others. It was very hard for me I'm not a stone but I did my duty. General Gutsby himself pinned on my second blue stripe. I was proud but I still feel bad. The General said I would set an example for you and others.

Hail to our country.

Your brother,

Michael

Dear Michael,

I read your letter. How could you kill Poppa? Maybe you killed Momma too. You better not. I want to grow up and leave here. Then I will kill you.

Your brother,

Charles

S.

For a month after they killed Poppa I sat like a gravestone. A Guard said, "Eat, they don't want you dead." I got very thin. My body told me, "Live." I thought of Charles. The disinfectant began to burn my skin. Maybe the doses got stronger. Something seemed different in the Camp. I guessed there was a labor shortage. One day the Guard came in and took me to my old bunk. I couldn't believe it. They let me have a real shower with real soap and a towel, a fresh mock, slippers, and hairwrap. My hair was growing back.

I'm in the room alone. I got used to solitude. Dozie is with Moira and they seem to get along. He waved to me a couple of times in the cafeteria. I was afraid to wave back. Why? That's what I wondered. Afraid for myself somehow but afraid of getting Dozie into trouble. Also I didn't want Moira to think I was waving at her. Why not? So I waved at them. Every day this little wave and wave back. My old friends! I blushed at my plate of pale blobs (the food was getting worse) embarrassed remembering Dozie. His voice reassuring me. The pressure of his naked body against mine. Lucky Moira. Yes shameful thoughts, oddly comforting. No one to answer to. No Momma no Joseph no Grandpa. Lonely yet free.

I like having the room to myself. A luxury. The cafeteria is my only Privilege so I appreciate little things. Sugar in my coffee. Extra helpings when permitted and palatable. The sly greetings. My wild thoughts.

Something happened to Till. Different rumors. He was demoted to the new Tunnel Duty. People say they found him one night half-eaten up with no insides or blood—sort of a hollow corpse. They put me back into the microbe unit but it's smaller now. There's a new Supervisor keen on caution and rules. We work in silence.

I think of poor Poppa. We are back at the house talking in our room. A solace this talk. I touch my cheek with his fingers. Sometimes I rebuke him. Why did we try to run away? Then he looks so miserable I rebuke myself. I remember how brave he was and hold on to that. I think of his terrible pain. He must have seen Michael marching in with the Firing Squad aiming at him. Most nights I still hear the shooting. I keep seeing it, wanting to make it into a nightmare. Somebody else's son. His own father.

I don't want to hate Michael but I do. If I favored Charles—yes I did. But Michael was different from the beginning. Not a cuddly baby. Hated to be held. Hand in mine like an eel slipping out of my grasp. Where else was I wrong? I loved both my sons. I loathe all killing now. Enemies enemies! Without breath without faces. Targets. Aren't they human beings? With runny noses? Afraid of us and wanting to live? With families?

I think of my wedding day and my white dress and the wedding trip to Niagara Falls. Water and sky. The roaring water. Birds. Trees in sunlight. Nature was strong then. Will it survive? Will it be there when I go Upside? Will I ever get there? Alive?

You must be taller now, Charles. If only I could see you. They won't let me write you or receive letters. Do you know I'm alive? Maybe the rules will change one day. Things seem tenser now, nearly sloppy except for the Lab. Guards are distracted. So much to do with fewer people. National Honor List selections will come up again. More people needing to be trained.

Our new Captain is lazy and on the way to getting fat. He loads his tray in the cafeteria and eats candy all the time. Must be taking bribes. He wants a leave but the Camp is in an emergency and I don't think anybody gets leaves anyway. People are on the lookout for tiny animals a few have seen.

I cherish the rest of my notebook to write in. I write secretly and hide my notes though no one pays much attention to me. Perhaps Michael's position keeps me from execution. I refuse to be grateful. So I talk to Poppa, to Charles in the future. To myself. Even to Michael.

People tend to shy away from me. I'm forbidden to talk about the tunnel or my escape attempt. Campers keep disappearing. At least one was a target in the Game Room and another in the Yard. People guess about the others.

The labor shortage increases. People are uneasy and real low all the time now. I hear the Love Room is so wild some Campers are afraid to go there. Too many fights. Sometimes something gets into a missile and they have to take the whole mechanism apart. Cradles aren't filled up the way they used to be. The Disinfection Campaign had to be cut back because people kept getting sick from the chemical spray and the cleaning agents.

Once when I was in the assembly line, a pale little creature scurried past my feet toward the wall of missiles. I wasn't frightened. I welcomed it. A renegade! Another time one lingered at my feet as if recognizing me. It was dark in color like those of the tunnel. The creature began shedding its skin and pulled it over its head with clawlike forepaws and sucked it into its jaws. The colorless new body was nearly invisible. I drew my foot back. The animal dashed toward the missiles. A marvel of adaptation! My compatriot. My fellow outcast.

What will come to pass will do so in its time. We may be overrun by the creatures. They may get bigger. Succeed us on earth. The next step.

I keep still about my observations. I've learned to be patient, to listen to myself, to my own common sense that struggles to be heard. I think I can hear it. It tells me to keep going.

THE CAVE

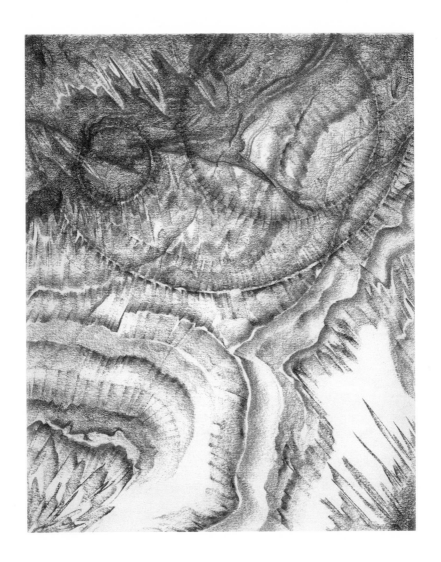

one   Burns

When he came to this dumb town I knew he meant trouble, but hell! anything woulda been an improvement in this wooden asshole of a place. A real Main Street, Boresville capital of Doris Daylight-Saving-Archie Bankerland. The kind of place you're born in or burn in, forget about visit. Me with my nowhere big ideas, never telling the whole bunch of them to fuck off. What a bunch of stiffs with their nice little kaffeeklatsch society you'd want to smash the dishes of. The kind of snot you wouldn't want up your nose. So we called the guy "Duke," which was what he called himself, and though some wanted his pedigree and shit before they'd give him the time on their Mickey Mousetrap watches, I size up the dude and think, "Thank holy crap you're not a squid like the rest."

He looked different. A good-looking guy, but that's not what I mean because I'm not a friggin faggot and he coulda been a bowwow for all I cared. But he always talked like he'd just been somewhere important, not exactly that but like he was gonna *do* something important. That was it. And even if he didn't do anything, you felt that he *could*. Maybe it was in his eyes—that power, a little like me, my funny eyes, a speckled sort of brown—a chick once told me she saw yellow light in them. But Duke—he has blue eyes, the kind with tiny black pupils that disappear when he's mean-mad, the kind that stupidstitious people wear a blue bead against. I guess I liked to walk down the street with him. People stared, they stare at anything that don't look like some tacky department-store dummy. We're different: he's tall, a Sylvester Stallooney-build type, except he's more kraut-looking than guinea, and with those pointy Texas-looking boots and spurs—those evil spurs would get the folks—and me, a runty guy with a head I shave sometimes and wearing Army boots I can kick ass with. Their asses, I mean.

Duke liked brown a lot and laughed saying he was a brownshirt, like the Nazis, but he wasn't part of that stupid shit. Duke was free. He didn't have dumb scruples about anything, and though he kept tight about his past, he once told me he killed a man in a fight and you couldn't feel free until you could cough up your conscience and spit it out. He said it took guts not to care and he talked about Hamlet, he was smart like that. "Conscience doth make cowards of us all!" He liked it when I quoted him and he'd laugh in a hoarse, choking sort of way that said there was a whole friggin bunch of things he could tell and didn't give shit about. He'd buy me drinks—he knew I didn't make much in the slaughterhouse where I handled the paperwork. One time he was feeling good about something, maybe won a bet or made a killing in the stock market and he says, "Drinks up and down the bar!" He buys a round for every creep there. A standup guy. A real prince.

When you look back at your life and it tastes like a mouthful of crud well you had your mouth open sometime when it shoulda been shut. I mean things begin somewhere and I'm trying to get it together in my head. Maybe if Duke and me had just stayed bending our elbows at Stu's Bar tanking up nice and easy on that hot Saturday afternoon things mighta been different. But shit, we don't make the world and it happens to us anyway.

So there was a guy there talking about some weirdo preacher who was going to do his God number after the high school baseball game, some freak from the Midwest where the corn grows natural from toejam to eyebrows and every damn place. No mention even in the chickenshit town paper where a cow's gas pains made Page One. Somebody had tied a couple of signs around a lamppost a few days before. Then somebody pulled them down real quick and that was that. Yeah, a real PR blitz. A Madison Avenue/Billy Graham/Maharishi fuckin snowjob. Ha! But this guy at the bar said he was going and there was just Duke and me left downing a couple more beers and it sounded like we could have some fun. Baseball was the heart of Boresville, the rabbit brain of Boresville. Football never made it big in this town though sometimes the team was worth watching because a kid would take a chance and hurt somebody or get hurt bad. Football was a real game. Anyway nothing could make it big here. *Nothing* was big here. I mean, nothing was BIG, ha!

So we go down the street with its doobeydoo Dutch elms the town fathers mothers and motherfuckers cared so much about you'd think their damn families were lining Main Street. Hell! What a fuss they'd make if a friggin tree got sick! That was even worse than the cow's gas pains. The carrying on the tree surgeons lopping off branches the prayers going up like crazy in church. They talked about Dutch elm disease like it was bubonic plague and rats were eating the babies. Shit.

Then they really got something to whine about—Lyme disease. They had these cute little signs around, "Deer Crossing," like the deer could read and would obey. When they found out the animals carried nice little ticks that made a whole lot of people sick—on their own friggin property no less—now that made Page One. I laughed because Nature was sticking it to them. They drove fast and smacked into deer on the road and I laughed when the animals could make the cars crash even when they were getting it. There was a hunting season and the rifles came out and you had to duck if you were lucky. They like their friggin rifles too and fancy outfits like they were after big game in Boolaboola Land, Africa. Shit!

We get to the playing field. The game was over. There weren't but a few dozen people in the stands. A tall, hungry-looking guy in a white suit was standing on a little platform over the pitcher's mound making a speech. The dude from Stu's was there next to another guy at the edge of the benches. They were both diggin the heavenly email real attentive and interested. Some teenyboppers were sitting up front getting religion with their asses hanging out of their shorts. Also some middle-aged and mostly old people.

"I beheld the earth and lo, it was without form, and void, and the heavens, and they had no light.

"I beheld the mountains, and, lo, they trembled, and all the hills moved lightly.

"I beheld, and, lo, there was no man, and all the birds of the heavens were fled."

So help me, this is what the guy was saying and it was straight from the Bible, couldn't you puke? Duke and I look at each other. I thought he was going to bust. It was just like we bumped into a talking clown.

People were listening, though. The sun was getting lower behind the preacher. I remember how he rolled his eyes like he was on this hotline to heaven and he was telling the folks. Then he got to "I beheld, and, lo, the fruitful place was a wilderness, and all the cities thereof were broken down at the presence of the Lord, and by his fierce anger." He looked all shook up the way they get at prayer meetings and some places when what they really want is a piece of ass and they end up with the Holy Ghost.

"Garbage!" I look at Duke. The word flies out of him like a catcher's throw back to the pitcher. A wild throw that hits the preacher in the gut. Even I'm surprised because I didn't know how angry Duke was or if he was just having fun. I guess both.

"Garbage!" he repeats. This time he cups his hands around his mouth. Duke sure could make a lot of noise when he wanted to. Then the guy from the bar turns around and says just as clear, "You shut up." The fat was out of the can.

"Talking to me?" says Duke. He starts toward the man. I take his arm trying to steer him away, telling him these were a bunch of dumb fanatics and we ought to make tracks. The odds were bad, and the only long shots I ever played were at an OTB. But he shakes free like a horse twitching off a fly.

"Yeah, I'm talking to you. Let the preacher preach."

Duke puffs up. Just got bigger right there like a genie out of a bottle. "He's talking crap and so are you," he says. The preacher was going on about the desolate land and shit. When he said, "The whole city shall flee," Duke shouts, "Damn right if you keep on talking!" A couple of people snickered but the tough from Stu's grabs him by the arm. "Listen, asshole—"

Well, nobody has a chance to listen to anything. Duke smashes the guy in the face and he staggers back. His friend jumps Duke with a tackle. Somebody yells for a cop and I land a rabbit punch on the tackler and give him a nice karate kick in the gut. Somebody starts screaming the preacher keeps on preaching like a karaoke singer people rush down from the stands to get a better look at the fight and then somebody grabs me from behind choking me till I'm halfway to hell. Next thing I remember is this friend of Duke's, Con Peters, and a cop bending over me. The two punks did a houdini.

Duke comes over rubbing his side. He and Con ask me how I feel. The cop asks what happened.

"Outsiders making trouble," says Duke. "Heckling the preacher." Nobody sticks around to make like witnesses. The fun was over. That's all, folks.

Cop scribbles in his notebook and walks away. The preacher shuts up shop and clears out. He looked tiny when he got off the platform. His two seedy flunkeys folded it up and the three of them made tracks.

Con (his tightass name was Constant) invites us to his house like he was the Red Cross. Duke says sure and they both help me to the car. My neck hurts like hell all the way up the hill. We drive through the goddamn elms and oaks to this real classy part of town where people would take me for the delivery boy. You could be a hundred years old here and if you were scruffy-looking and carrying a package you were a boy. Wear a uniform, deliver the mail, you could be a man. Nifty place.

The last time I was there was high school. I got invited to one graduation party by this far-out kid who got stoned a lot and her father was a vet. Plenty of dogs and cats in the town so he did a good business. I musta been early. Her mother was on the way out and she looked at me like she had stepped in poodleshit. The dog was barking and she asks me through the screen was I delivering something. I was going to say, "Yes, lady, a time bomb," but I choked up and the kid came to the door with me just standing there like a spaz. I hand her a box of candy.

"The Heights" they call that section. Duke calls it "Heights of Folly" but he likes to be invited just the same even if he just goes to laugh. He laughs at everybody. Money people—he felt easy with them maybe because he felt superior to that kind. He had dough and didn't give shit about it. He was after other things. Sometimes I wondered why he hung out with me. I'd feel like a pet monkey or an orangutan making him look good. But he didn't really need that. I remember a school trip to a museum. There was this Spanish king and his family and right smack up front was this dwarf all decked out fine as shit and smiling like he swallowed a lump of gold. So a king could keep a dwarf for fun and though I was no dwarf I always say that Duke was a prince.

two   Flora

Years ago—a hundred, maybe?—I recall my mother, Abby Young, telling Charles, my father, that Con had proposed to me. She asked him whether I ought to accept and he said, "Yes!" loud and clear. That question and that answer will ring in my ears to my grave. Wrong question, wrong answer. Wrong everything. Con was a decent sort of person who thought because he sold insurance he might be Wallace Stevens. An amiable kind of guy who brings stray cats home and then you have to feed them and give them away. We didn't have any children though we were still young enough, but we'd reached the point where people stopped asking. I had a tilted womb. Things could be done, especially with couples who had an active sex life. We didn't. We were settling into his being my baby, so that probably made me his mother, which worked out neatly after his mother died. There I was, the handy replacement. We probably should have adopted children, but we had the town strays: dogs, cats, people.

And there was my older sister Mary, too-long-divorced, with Maybelle and Roy, her teenage kids Con could play daddy to. Mary loved that. Maybe she hoped—unconsciously, of course—that I'd break my pelvis or something (the pelvis wasn't that necessary, but she didn't know) so Con could play husband, too. I hate to seem uncharitable, but it happens sometimes. In the best of families.

Anyway, we'd also had goldfish, a tropical aquarium, white mice (a temporary martyrdom; I loathe mice). Creatures would come and go, grow and die and be replaced. For a while I tried community work and even considered getting into local politics, but then I'd receive calls at dinnertime and Con would get upset. We'd be eating by candlelight in the dining room, just the two of us, with some of that nonstop Beethoven playing on the stereo. We'd have the Fifth Symphony with the chocolate pud-

111

ding or Swedish meatballs or chicken soup; the Ninth would come over the banana bread or roast beef. We'd talk about my father's latest operation (hemorrhoids), or Mary's root canal work, her financial distress (chronic), choosing a college for Maybelle and Roy. I might have cared to listen to *Don Giovanni*, the Beatles' early, shimmering innocence ("I Wanna Hold Your Hand"), Aretha Franklin, or the news. I might have wished instead (occasionally) to sit by myself in front of the television set and eat my dinner watching the evening news, maybe call an old friend. But we dined in a civilized sort of way that people envied, and I'd just be grateful it wasn't a dinner party with a dozen of Con's friends from the office. I guess all our friends were really Con's—I wasn't a gregarious type. Most of those from the office made me feel awkward. I couldn't tell jokes and felt like an outsider. I guess I didn't especially like them. So I didn't mind Con's having Duke over a few times. Duke was a little strange—"mysterious" is the word—but he was a refreshing change from the office crowd.

We had had a beautiful wedding and went to live in a beautiful old two-story white frame house ever after, not exactly in ecstasy but pleasantly enough. Everybody told me I was lucky—Con was good-looking, kind, had a steady job, didn't drink to excess, didn't gamble or chase women. Everyone was happy at our wedding, his mother, my parents, everyone, so it was obviously a good thing to have done.

I like gardening, keep a flower bed in front and grow a few vegetables in the back. We have a nice picnic table and benches out back with a latticed canopy of grapevines. We kept the swing that was there when we moved in. A silent reminder. Adoption would really make things permanent, wouldn't it? I doubt we ever will, but there's still time.

Of all the rooms in our three-bedroom house, I like the dining room best. It's elegant, almost—English mahogany things picked up at auctions, a good copy of a Sheraton sideboard on the left, with a big gilt mirror over it, silver in the drawers, silver put away into tarnish-proof bags (I hate polishing silver—dull as brushing your teeth), books and records in the bookcase on the right, built by Con and Charles (my husband mostly supplied the labor, my father, the lumber), cherished books I wished I could have crawled into long ago and disappeared into my real life which, once upon a time, was wanting to be a writer. I'd stand at the French doors, near the fringe of the Oriental carpet with its rich scarlet and blues, and look across the table at the venetian blinds and gold draperies behind Con's empty chair, remembering a poem by a New York writer in a book about her neighborhood.

I've been ringed with napkins
unfolded with linens
presented upon china
in crystal
candlesticks used.

Used. Used up? Was that me, Flora Peters? Flora Young Peters? Flora Not-so-Young, Not-Getting-Any-Younger Peters? Wife of Constant, the Rock? And then I'd think about him, sweet, a little bumbly sometimes, yet there for me always, somebody to turn to, somebody to attend plays and cultural events with (there was a college town about twenty miles away), someone who needed me. Once in awhile I wondered whether he felt a little short-changed, too, but I'd turn away quickly from that one. And then I'd take this yawning hole of a heart, this yearning, gawking, gaping, empty shopping-bag of feelings and say, Yes, here I am, this is what I'm good for.

We were between seasons with the pets. Reprieve time. So on Saturday Con went out to make a loyal appearance at a friend's garage (read "junk") sale and pass by the high school baseball game. I stayed home reading a book. He was late for our early dinner. We were going to catch the seven o'clock movie in town, something politely pornographic, "R" instead of "X" rated. When he appeared with Duke and this stranger, a stocky Brando-out-of-*Streetcar* type, I didn't feel annoyed, just sort of— interested.

They came in the back door and there I was at my station in the kitchen. Con apologized for being late. He introduced the man as Burns, and right away I had this funny feeling, as if something from his intense, Al Pacino eyes sort of settled into mine. He wore a white T-shirt with

"BURNS" stamped on it. I liked that because he wasn't advertising anyone or anything but himself. Duke removed his ten-gallon hat, but Burns didn't have to remove anything. He had a stubble of black hair, his bare arms and his chest were muscular, his jeans were sculpted as if he lived in Levis and went swimming in them.

"There was trouble at the preacher's meeting after the game. Burns got hurt in the neck—maybe we ought to put something on it. Duke took a few punches, too—"

Duke protested that he was fine and we all went into the living room.

I examined Burns's injury. He had red welts below his left ear. He winced at my touch and kept looking at me. I soaked a hand towel in warm water and wrapped it like a collar around his neck, with a larger towel below it to catch any moisture. Con went to get drinks. The men had scotch, I took sherry. Duke always looked at me in a nice way, appreciating a woman, but his companion's gaze was different.

I sipped my drink slowly and sat with the men while they talked about the silly preacher and the people getting so excited about nothing at all. I had this feeling that Burns was looking at me—how can I describe it?—not insolently but intimately. He sat in the elegant wing chair, engulfed by its tapestry. He should have been sitting in the black leather chair that Con liked and Duke sat in when he came over. It blended with the boots and spurs he sometimes affected. Thank God he didn't dig his heels into the leather ottoman!

I was wearing shorts, not short shorts but regular length (years ago they only permitted the modest Bermuda length in town). I have a pretty good figure. An image of Burns and me sitting there stark naked popped into my head. A psychiatrist might have said it was wishful thinking, but I don't have a shrink. Most people around here still think you've got to be a little crazy to go. It wouldn't do your business any good and it would be hazardous to your job.

I asked them to stay for dinner, taking (but not needing) my cue from Con, so we didn't go to the movies. Con put Beethoven's Fifth on the stereo. Sinatra singing "Strangers in the Night" might have been more appropriate.

Except for the food and conversation and what I was feeling and maybe what Burns was feeling, we could have been sitting at a concert in church.

Duke had traveled quite a bit. He never told us exactly what he did. We knew that he traveled a lot on business and that he had made a great deal of money. He lived rather simply in a small house and didn't seem to have many—if any—visitors, though he sort of exuded money. It was like an animal smell that other animals could pick up, a smell you were comfortable with. Last time he brought over a bottle of vintage French champagne. I kept the bottle as a souvenir. After I changed into a skirt, I set the table in the dining room, using linen napkins and our best silver from the sideboard. I announced dinner.

I'd prepared chicken and rice and a salad. I liked the way Burns dug right in. When I offered a bunch of paper napkins to hold the chicken legs with, Burns said, "No, thanks," and went on eating. He wasn't a slob or anything, just determined to do it his own way. I liked that, too.

The door knocker clacked noisily and I got up. In the doorway stood Abby and Charles, my parents, looking hectic.

"Did you hear? Did you hear?" they kept saying. Con came over.

"We were on our way to the new restaurant," Abby began. "We had the car radio on—I'm glad we had it fixed—"

"We got this terrible news flash," my father broke in. "All the governors have been rushed to the Capitol. Some godforsaken island near Greece has been invaded by somebody. Any minute now, we may be at war!" He was out of breath.

Duke walked over, then Burns who was wiping his hands with his napkin. End of dinner party.

"The President is going on television to talk to the country," Charles continued. We'd better see what's happening." Any excuse to watch TV, I thought reflexively.

Constant said we should call Mary and the kids. Mom rushed to the phone. Nobody home. Everybody gathered in the living room. The TV image was clear. On the screen, a reporter was interviewing a familiar official who looked resolutely impassive. Like the newscasters who withheld reactions to their news, except maybe sports. Disaster, death, weather—weather had the edge.

"Governor," said the reporter, "How do you think the President will respond to the bombing of Anticleia?"

Our governor brushed back a lock of wavy white hair. His speech went something like this, the one from Column A or B, the one you didn't get dessert with.

"It's not for any of us to say. However, in this great country of ours, the decision of one person cannot supersede majority rule. That is what our forefathers planned, and that is why we are the superpower we are today." Burns was holding his stomach. We glanced at each other.

"I and all the other governors are gathered here at the request of the President. He has the information, and he'll let us know what he expects us to do in the emergency."

"Then you admit there is a state of emergency?"

"You used the word. I say the situation is serious, but the extent is yet to be determined by the President and the legislators. Make no mistake, it is the people who will ultimately determine the measures to be taken. I stand here as a public servant of my constituents, nothing more."

Burns and I groaned. Duke and Con shook their heads. My parents looked grim.

"Have you anything to say to the people of your State?"

"To the people of my State I say this: Have faith! Faith in your leaders! Faith in your democratic government! Faith in yourselves! Faith in God! And may God help us all."

Burns laughed. Duke held his head. Con and I wondered how anything so serious could come out so funny. My father was irritated—by us. Mother's scowl underscored his displeasure.

While the reporter was thanking the governor, Abby fretted about Mary. Then the image switched to a flag-draped room where the President sat, staring directly over an endless desk. He smiled in response to a signal, then dropped the expression and began to read a statement.

"My fellow countrymen and women," he declared in a gravelly voice,

"I come to you with a heavy heart today. Our friends, our allies, the peaceful, hardworking, God-fearing natives of the sovereign island of Anticleia have been attacked, I repeat, attacked by our common Enemy. This evil deed was committed by evil people. They hate peace. They hate good people. They envy us because we are strong and successful, because we are a democracy. Let me be clear. The attackers are not guerrillas engaged in civil war. They are terrorists, trained by the Enemy, armed by the Enemy, and they represent a foreign ideology. We are committed to the defense of our friends. We have been patient, because we are peaceful. For months we have had reports of hostile activity in and around Anticleia. We know from our forefathers—and mothers—that eternal vigilance is the price of liberty. We have not been deceived. Our naval maneuvers in the area have been menaced twice in recent weeks by enemy aircraft. The unprovoked, vicious attack on this innocent island violates all international and moral law, the laws of God and man, and threatens the lives of our military advisers stationed there. We will avenge the sacrifices they have made.

"As your President, by the power invested in me by the people and the laws of our Homeland, and in order to fulfill our military commitment to Anticleia, I have instructed our land, sea, and air capabilities to aid our noble friends. Toward their defense—and our own—we are now engaged in a limited bombing action against the air base from which this evil attack was launched. This base, which lies on the Enemy's mainland, must be destroyed. Only by such action can we reaffirm, clearly and immediately, our sacred and unswerving pursuit of peace and our shared purpose on earth with all men and women of good will.

"I call upon each and everyone of you to join me in prayer for our Homeland in these perilous days. Let us remain united and strong, proud of our past, vigilant in our present, and hopeful for the future of decent people everywhere. God bless us everyone. Thank you."

"I feel sick," said Abby. Dad put his arm around her.

"Me, too," said Burns. "Fire and brimstone. Ha! We'd better get ready for it."

"It looks very serious," said Con.

"We can't let anyone push us around," said Duke. "Where the hell is Anticleia, anyway?"

"I think it's in Homer," I ventured.

"Homer? Oh, yes. *The Odyssey* and all that. Heroes and wars. Good for the economy," Duke remarked.

"Anticleia was a woman. Odysseus' mother, I'd guess."

"You ever try a quiz show?" asked Burns. Duke laughed with him. Chauvinists, I concluded.

"Bombing their mainland is an act of war," Con was saying. "Both sides have nuclear weapons. This could start a war."

"Nuclear war!" said Charles. "My God—where would we go? I told you," he snapped at Con, "I told you bomb shelters were a good idea!" Dad for the jugular, with a spoon. "All you could do was heckle the governor with your picket signs and a bunch of troublemakers. Now see what we've got!"

"Oh, Dad!" I couldn't let him attack Con—with me thrown in. "It was a dumb idea then and it has nothing to do with now!"

"We've already had that discussion," said Con quietly. Had we ever. I was grateful for his patience. A good son-in-law. When the regular program came back on, he turned off TV and resumed Beethoven's Fifth.

"Can't we listen to something else?" I said.

So we got Nat King Cole singing "Stay as Sweet as You Are." Though we both like golden oldies, the circumstances were pretty sour.

My mother dialed Mary again and returned, looking miserable. "She's still not home."

I suggested drinks and brought in a tray with glasses, ice, and soda. Setting them on the little bar beside the bottles Con had brought in, I cheerfully invited, "Help yourselves, folks."

Con got up to play host.

"People need faith," my father expounded. "Plain, old-fashioned faith," he emphasized, waving his J&B on the rocks.

Duke turned to him. "You might have liked the preacher at the ball field this afternoon." He knew how to scrape a conversation off the floor.

"You mean Jeremiah, the doom and gloom guy." Charles brightened to the topic. "I've seen him around. Our minister invited him to attend service on Sunday, but he refused. An odd bird if you ask me."

"Maybe he wanted to preach a sermon."

"Preach! I heard about him. All that scary stuff. And wearing a white suit. Long hair, too. That guy would drive the few folks we've got left right out the door. Life is depressing enough. People go to church to lift their spirits."

"You mean they want entertainment," Duke mused.

"Damned right! We've got a good fellow now. Tells some jokes. Reaches the people. Gives them hope that things will turn out OK, eventually."

I couldn't keep still. "Maybe they should just go to the movies."

"Flora!" Now my mother was upset.

"You've got a point, sir," said Duke, helpfully. "It ought to be a capital offense to be gloomy in bad times. Who needs that? Besides, the guy was a bore. A phony, I swear. Ought to string him up."

"Oh," said Charles. "I wouldn't go that far."

"I would," Duke persisted. "Look at Dante. He put the Hypocrites way down in Hell. I say, string the guy up!"

While it was heaven to hear someone refer to Dante, I was uncomfortable with Duke's vehemence.

"You're exaggerating to make a point," Con said tactfully, making his own point.

"No," Duke insisted. I mean it. Maybe not string him up, shoot him. Execute him. Publicly."

"You're not serious."

"Like slicing off the soft spot on a peach. You have to be cool about it."

"The preacher may be wrong," Con insisted, "but he thinks his message is hopeful. He's warning people that they'd better change. You can't kill him for making a mistake."

"I don't tolerate fools," Duke said icily. "In my business, I can't afford to."

"What business?" from Charles.

"I'm retired," Duke replied, closing the subject. I was getting to hate parties. Maybe it was the drinks.

Abby kept dialing Mary and getting more agitated. And then the knocker banged and Con went to the door. Mary collapsed neatly into his arms.

It was Mary who gave us the latest breaking news. Our country's West Coast had been bombed while we were having drinks and listening to Nat King Cole. We were at war for real. She was at a friend's and got hysterical and drove to the beach to look for Maybelle and Roy. They had gone off with their friends, Jack and his sister Julia, and God knows what they were up to. This from Mary. Since she had to be father and mother, she did doubles for both, and there was Con tossed in—no, tossing himself in as a spare. I loved my sister, I was brought up that way, but I wasn't a fool. If I had felt more intensely about my husband I might have minded more, but she still triggered my sense of a territorial imperative. Talk about invasions!

"There's no point in looking for them blindly," Con soothed. "They might be on their way here. Have you called Jack and Julia's house?"

"Nobody's there." Then she and Abby were hugging each other. I couldn't win.

"Your children are certainly intelligent," Duke soothed. "How old are they?"

"Maybelle is sixteen and Roy is eighteen. They're babies!"

"They'll have sense enough to phone or go home or come here."

"What will they do?" Mary moaned.

"The question is," Duke went on, "what are *we* going to do?"

His point was so sensible that it shut everybody up. Dad agreed, Burns, of course, and then Con, too. Abby was too busy consoling Mary, but even I got the point. Somebody turned on TV again and Nat King Cole stopped singing.

We got a nice picture of the American flag. I recalled my parents once being wary of color TV with its radiation seepage and all—what a laugh, now! Somebody was singing "The Star-Spangled Banner" as if it were *Aida*. Then a voiceover announced: "Due to the national emergency, the broadcasting of regular programs has been temporarily suspended. Please stay tuned to this station for music and up-to-the-minute news. Thank you." No commercial. Apparently everyone had run like hell. Con flipped channels with the remote. Snow. Or just dark. I brought in a radio from the kitchen. We got music (the fiddling of Nero?) and swatches of silence.

"What's happening? Where can we hide?" wailed Abby. That was the nitty-gritty. She was OK, full tilt at survival.

"Not the cellar," said Charles. "The house could burn and cave in. We'd be done for."

"To a crisp," said Duke.

"Say," Burns told my father. "You gimme an idea." He hesitated. "I don't know who else might be thinking the same thing."

"Tell us!" Abby pleaded.

"Charley's right," he continued. "The cellar would make a nice barbecue pit. But there's a place, one place in this whole freakin town where we could go. It's locked in, got a door, and there's an underground stream for water. It's down in the ground, and rocky, like a fort—"

"You mean the Cave," said Con.

"Yup. Better the Cave than caved in, I say." He was triumphant with his idea.

"It's town property," Charles mused. "There's supposed to be a security guard at the entrance even though it's been closed down. No money in it."

"He's probably not there now, under the circumstances," from Duke.

"Suppose he—or somebody else—is there," my father insisted.

"Duke and I can scare them off," Burns volunteered.

"How?"

"Whips and chains!" laughed Burns.

"I have guns," said Duke quietly.

"Guns?" asked my father.

"It was my business," snapped Duke. So that was it, I thought. Not "business" as in "mind your own," but "business" as in commerce. Amazing—everybody seemed sort of relieved, including me. As if we had a good shepherd who would take care of us and blow up anybody who interfered. A man who could take charge.

"We might have to hunt, too," Charles remarked supportively.

"I'm not going anywhere without my children!" from Mary.

"Leave a note on the door for them," said Burns. "No—better leave it inside, so no one will follow us." Smart. Discreet.

"Mary's right," said Con. "We can't leave without the kids." We! Uncle Con to the rescue.

"There's a war on and we need to find shelter—for everybody." I don't know how that sounded when I was actually thinking, "We need to run for our lives!" I wasn't even thinking like an aunt. I kept hearing Con siding with Mary, even if we all had to fry for it.

"We've got to move fast," said Duke quickly. "Otherwise Burns and I will leave you folks to work it out." They could go and lock us all out. My survival mechanism was in high gear. Like my parents'.

"Duke's right," I was relieved to hear my father say. "We'll all have to claim the Cave right away. Like pioneers." He got things on track.

We made plans. Burns and Duke would go to Duke's house and get guns and supplies, then pass by Burns's house, beyond the railroad tracks, on the way to the Cave. Mary, Mother, and Dad would go home to pick up a few things. I made a couple of calls—of course the stores were closed. Con and I would pack some items. We had bottled water, cartons for food—canned, dried, powdered. The Government had scared us before like this, and I had learned the lesson of preparedness. We were all to meet at the Cave in a half-hour or so, about six-thirty. Suddenly they were gone, leaving me with a head full of Sterno, batteries, toilet paper, the finer accessories of modern life.

"I'm not so sure about what we're doing," Con told me. "I wish Roy and Maybelle were here already." I wanted to scream. It was hard enough to think clearly—which items to take, how much or how many of each. I was becoming shaky as the reality sank in: the prospect of uprooting our lives, facing chaos, even death.

"Don't you dare!" I warned. "Don't lay any of your second thoughts on me. I can't handle you and me at the same time."

"Suppose a neighbor came by—"

"There won't be enough room. We decided that."

"Duke and Burns decided that."

"Well, somebody has to decide something!"

"Flora, it could turn into a free-for-all. Dog eat dog. Anarchy."

"You have a better idea? Spare me the philosophy."

"Sarcasm won't help."

"Maybe nothing will help except a kick in the pants."

"Vulgarity won't help, either."

I couldn't take it. "What about the obscenity of making war, of 'calculated losses' and 'collateral damage,' you and me as statistics nobody will ever count anyway? Who gives a shit about us except us? Oh, why don't you go help Mary? I don't need a heckler." I hated my words even as they bubbled out.

"It's a little late now."

How I detested his irony. "Damn it!" We melted down into silence as we continued packing.

"Did you lock all the windows and close the doors?" I said finally, as if we'd been preparing for a vacation.

"Yes. I'll turn off the water."

"The hot water heater, too."

Civility restored, we got out of there.

three   Jeremiah

 It was a bust, a God-awful bust, praise God. Dingy little turnout and with that commotion in the stands Martha and John couldn't even take up a collection. A disaster! I wanted to blame everything on the disturbance but there was no way I could fool myself. The humiliation—Humiliation!—when I asked for worshippers to come down from the stands to me. "Make your peace with God! Make your peace with God!" The paltry response upset me so much that my mind kept changing "peace" to "piece"—a switch right straight from the Devil. The Devil was speaking to me quite a bit lately. I was having impulses—to smoke a joint, get drunk, sleep with a whore, get syphilis, even AIDS. I needed to abase myself, prove I understood I was just no good, a futile case, a clown in a white suit. I could break my heart with laughter.

The white suit. Martha's idea of salesmanship, a trademark. To me it was just hard to keep clean. Martha insisted on washing my things, including the suit—its fabric was synthetic (like the message?)—but I drew the line at my underwear and socks. Still, it was a nuisance. It also made me a good target for an assassin, though who would want to take me off the scene? Nobody even knew who I was! Jeremiah Thomas Whitney. Inventor of the cotton gin? A financier? A museum? A nothing, praise God! A cipher. Zero minus. I walked to the bench under a tree, brooding, hoping Martha and John would think I was meditating and leave me alone.

"Jeremiah?" That timid soprano. No, Martha would not leave me alone. We had quit the ball field and ridden in silence up the hill. I didn't want to go back to the trailer camp right away so John drove us to a quiet spot, somewhat overgrown, with trees like a little park. Martha joined me on the bench while John parked the van in the shade.

"Are you all right?"

"Yes, Martha." Oh yes, I'm fine. Going down the tubes in a tub, going down the waste pipe of my dreams like raw sewage. Martha, hollow-faced, gazed anxiously at me. I braced myself for her pious consolation.

"The baseball game was a hard act to follow," she began. "Maybe you should have accepted that invitation to visit the church." Martha trying not to sound reproachful.

"Maybe people missed the commercials they get on radio and TV. I think they missed the commercials today. Next time, you and John just go out there and shake it. Shake your bootie! Talk up the gig like you were selling snake oil medicine. I need to learn to sell God. Gotta have a sales pitch."

"Oh, Jeremiah," she whimpered.

"I could offer something—a free gift as it's known to the tribes of redundancy. A place in Heaven with hundred per cent down mattresses to lie on while listening to the music of the spheres."

I stopped, fearing Martha was going to cry. She was so tenderhearted, bless her. She moved closer and put her arm around my shoulder. John came over.

"What's going on?" Good old John to the rescue. "It weren't too bad," he said in his meekly stubborn way. "Thee had rotten luck with them muggers in the stands." John had spent a few months on a farm with a Quaker family before coming to the orphanage where the three of us met. He clung to the "thees" as the "thous" faded from his speech and presumably from his memory.

So here we were again, the happiness kids. Orphans all, conceived by a Holy Ghost of ill fortune. My parents were killed in a plane crash. They were going to the Bahamas for a few days without me—one of those bargain deals—and for years I felt the crash was my fault because I resented their leaving me behind with a babysitter. They loved each other and wanted to be alone for once, I guess. Who expected it to be forever? They figured they'd always be around till I grew up. There was no relative to drop me on, no cash, and the tiny bit of insurance went to the orphanage. Next case.

Martha's father got himself knifed to death in a barroom fight. Her mother had a weak heart and couldn't take the grief. Martha was a good child, rewarded for her pains by her mother's having a heart attack and drowning in the bathtub. As for John, his mother wanted to make a clean break of everything when she remarried. A real tidy person! The man had children of his own and she wanted a child with him. John's father took him for a while, then just evaporated. All that alcohol. The boy ended up in our orphanage, which wasn't a bad deal. Some of the nuns were decent to us. A few seemed like they were punishing us for our parents' sins—as if God had to get his innings.

God certainly got his from me. I was good, very good in prescribed ways—clasped my hands, sat up tall and straight in my seat, looked solemn. But then I was sensitive and saw things. I think it happened or started happening after I read the Book of Revelations. A wonderful book full of fire and animals and fantastic events. I had dreams of being in Heaven. Then I'd have dreams during the day. I told one of the sisters. They started keeping an eye on me. Sometimes I could bring on these visions at will. I'd go all dreamy and quiet and just stand wherever I was. It impressed everybody. It even impressed me. They started the interviews. I wasn't a Catholic though my mother was, and I sure as heck didn't want to be a priest. It meant that awful thing about staying away from girls. I liked girls a lot. Thinking about them would give me an erection and I'd have to sit down. It was easier in winter. I could wear a coat.

I was getting to know Martha as best I could under the surveillance. She was wild for affection then. I guess we all were. She had a rosy plump face and lips as if she'd been eating cherries. We'd walk around the grounds with our hands in each other's pockets, rubbing to beat the band. I guess we were what you'd call sexually precocious—aware anyway. No, I certainly did not want to be a priest. I knew I'd be something religious eventually, though, and Martha was my first follower. Then some long-lost relative claimed her and she had to leave the orphanage. We kept in touch. John joined us about eight or nine months before Martha left. He stayed on after me. He was the youngest—my second convert. I thought I was on my way. To glory, praise God.

Eventually we hooked up together in the outside world, the real world that stood our little orphanage values on their heads. We had to be acrobats. Most of the "good" we had learned was considered stupidity or at best, naïveté. Only the bad things mattered: getting sex, getting money, being macho (menacing and/or ready to kill), making war. Nobody got a prize for sewing on buttons the way little Martha did in the homemaking contest. She sewed shirts in a factory. She could have stitched up her backside, mouth, and navel and no one would give her a smile. Do your job, shut up, collect your paycheck and scram. You could live on top of a telephone pole. You could live at the bottom of a mine shaft with six kids eating anthracite. You could be irradiated from your job in a nuclear power plant and glow like a neon sign. Or you could be in jail pleading your innocence, smashed in the face day after day until you went blind and choked to death on your broken teeth. There was this—coldness. Everywhere—in business and the government, in families, freezing up the whole society. There was a need for something or someone who could pick it all up in two arms and say, "OK, brothers and sisters, hold on. Help is coming. I'm here." Maybe for me it was a kind of atonement—for that fierce anger with my parents I can still feel occasionally and then bitterly, bitterly regret. But I did start out liking people and wanting to help them. I still wanted to but was somehow screwing up the message. I understood how folks were messed up. Worse than me.

I found a job in the mailroom of a big company. I thought about what it meant, what I meant. I read my Bible and kept my eyes open. I listened to the radio and watched my secondhand television set, then pretty much gave up on both. Those radio preachers and rich televangelists right out of show business—none of them were saying what I wanted to say, even though I wasn't always sure exactly what that was or how I was supposed to say it. People seemed to expect a certain style and I started to go along with that, picking up from what I'd seen and heard. I thought that was OK because I knew deep down I was sincere. I was convinced people needed me. Like they were all dying and I could give them extreme unction. Or life. And because the real world had penetrated this far, I thought I could earn a living at it.

I gathered Martha and John. John wasn't doing well except he ate regularly in the greasy spoon where he washed dishes and tried to keep the cockroaches out of the soup. We got together for Bible readings. We talked and talked. For each of us the road became a way out and a way to something. I guess I became the road, too. Not just a detour ditching the sewn shirts cockroach soup and mail slots that never got past the alphabet, but a real dispensation. If that sounds like a pope, well, I *was* a kind of bishop. A vicar of Christ in my own way. And though I was miles from having a gang of twelve, two made a start. Except that I'd had the same and only two for years. We'd go into a town, pick up a few dollars at a few meetings then clear out. I didn't have any sense of roots going down. Sure, we'd get some names and the women liked me. It was a little hard on Martha, but if she didn't want to sweep up some crumbs of living on the way—well, that was her choice. I needed a woman once in awhile. I was kind of ashamed to think it was like fueling up the van.

The van! How we planned for it saved for it ate slept and dreamed it a million miles and back. We took extra jobs, we held little prayer meetings in storefronts. I stopped having visions in the daytime but the Virgin Mary would come to me in dreams and promise me a van. Martha and John were more impressed with me than ever. I felt they had too high an opinion of me and my so-called powers already. Sometimes, when their trust weighed heavily on me I'd want to tell them I was a fake just to shake them up. Maybe deep down I believed that myself.

It was hard being poor all the time. You couldn't hide hunger under your pillow except when you slept. I remember hearing my boss say, "He who sleeps, dines," and I'd want to shove his mail down his throat. Rich people—Jesus was right about them, praise God. Easier for a pregnant camel to go through the eye of a needle than for a rich man to crash the heavenly gates. He'd likely try to buy his way in. Probably was a mean penny-pinching bastard making his money in the first place. Or was Heaven a fairy tale of deferred payments to keep the poor in line? A damn good one for sure, that buoyed your spirits even while you were sinking in the mud. Daily life was mud, was muck. You needed clowns, fools, acrobats. You walked a tightrope all your life even though you couldn't see it.

Yet when you saw another man walking a tightrope there was—a recognition. Somebody in jeopardy. Somebody like me. I was a clown on a tightrope, holding a funny little umbrella I called Jesus. I fell a lot.

"We could have a picnic there," John was saying. How long had he been talking? He spoke slowly, hanging his words like wash on a clothesline. I hadn't missed much.

"Where?"

"That Cave I been telling you about. Down there."

"You and Martha go."

"I don't feel like—" she began.

"Go! I just want to sit here." I wished I didn't have to spell it out.

"OK, Jer." John was the only person who called me that. Amputated three-quarters of my name. I didn't care. It made him feel easier with me. Good old John. Dependably honest. Honestly dependable, a Fool of God you'd better be kind to because God works mysteriously. You better believe it, praise the Lord.

At last they left me alone. I watched them going down the hill. A spontaneous jaunt! What was spontaneous in my own life anymore except for a furtive bit of diversion? Sneaking off, not wanting to hurt poor Martha. That awful time she came back to the van. Surprise! I can still feel the shame. And the rest of it—the raggle-taggle three of us, like religious beatniks, scrounging up a few bucks on the road just to get by.

What was I preaching, anyway? Trying to scare people straight with visions of a dire future, like the man who said you could keep delinquents out of prison by taking them to visit jails? I believed the world had become a more and more terrible place—full of greed, violence, corruption of every sort. People needed to change their ways. Fast. Was I up to the task? Or merely holding up the scary carcass of religion and serving it half-baked? It was easier to offer rote exercises, cant. What people expected. Each occasion, each year was taking me farther away from my starting point, my truest self. From the simple text itself. Wasn't it about love, not fear? Love and forgiveness. I was out of touch—with myself, my deep-down self. With the message I was supposed to be delivering. The Heavenly Mail, like my old job but on a larger scale. I was a useless cynic. A dummy mouthing words. Who was the ventriloquist? Preaching all this stuff and scaring people's change out of their pockets and I couldn't even do that today. Was I any better than anybody, or was I venal like the rest? A poor man's televangelist? Was the whole deal about the damned collection basket? And "Salvation"—asking folks to believe, to do only that, forget about helping people on earth—wasn't that like a call to outer space? Wasn't it sort of—empty?

All I could do was keep going. Where? Where? I needed a sign.

I lay on the bench and turned on my little radio for some music. I thought about the end of the world.

four   Martha

"Thee be careful," said John, extending his hand. A sweet hand, a boy's hand. I could never believe he had washed all those dishes. I couldn't take his hand because if I did I'd collapse, howling my dumb heart out. We had been dismissed—I had been dismissed by Jeremiah like a schoolchild at three o'clock. He never wanted to be with us—with me anymore, not a bit more than he had to. The romance was over. No, it was a sort of one-night stand you had to keep living with. Oh, not quite that, I guess.

I loved Jeremiah, always, even after the other women (they pursued him), even after we went back to being "friends" and that raw, bloody pain had me screaming for days inside my head. My heart began to hurt so I'd take a drink if there was one around, or aspirin, or even antihistamine pills to make me drowsy—anything—when I really wanted to swallow nails and die. In front of him. At his feet. Bloody and foaming at the mouth, showing him what he'd done. No, I was doing it to myself. A psychologist might say I was very angry and wanted to hurt him, kill him, but how could I hurt Jeremiah when my wound was so fresh! In the last town, that redheaded girl with the white breasts you could see through her flimsy cotton blouse. He got rid of John and me for a few hours but we returned too soon and there he was. Hadn't even bothered to draw the privacy curtain I'd made. There he was, with the girl, in the same cot he and I had shared a long time ago, but it was ours ours ours. Before, when he'd made out, he'd be careful, consider my feelings, disappear for a while, and come back as if he'd been on some errand. But this was different. This was razorblades.

I fled with John. We went to a bar, hung out till evening without enough money to get drunk. When we went back there was a blond bobby-pin on the floor, an empty Tampax tube in the wastebasket. Whoreslob! Bitch! How could I feel so much rage and pain and stay alive? What was I doing there? Had my saint, my God, turned into a devil? Had God and the Devil got mixed up?

I wanted to believe in Jeremiah, in someone, find somewhere I could put my heart and soul to rest, so much affection there always it might burst out of me when I least expected it. If I weren't careful, it could land me in the gutter. Where had my Jeremiah gone? That wild, sweet boy with the crazy visions that got me going. He could see angels dancing on the head of a pin, he could see and say anything and I'd believe it. Believe! And fight anyone who questioned or doubted. Jeremiah was beyond doubt, beyond the moon! To feel so deeply about somebody then discover the clay feet of the marble statue—no, they weren't feet. They were paws. With thick claws. Bear claws to maul your soft and mushy heart. But the head—that statue's head! Shooting stars coming out of it, fire and frenzy coming out of it. That head had just gone away for now. It left the body, sometimes. I wanted the body, oh, yes. But the head put it all together. That head was playing hide and seek. A horror movie in real life.

Down the slope a few berry bushes crouched here and there, having yielded their fruit to the birds. Sunlight fell through the trees, dappling dead things underfoot: last year's leaves and twigs, small animals and birds that surely lay beneath them. Instead of this scrub oak and pine, the forest should have been denser, branches merging at the top like a canopy to shield and hide me. A tree lay ahead, recently fallen, its leaves green, yet spotted with blight.

"Let's sit here a minute," I told John.

"Thee is tired," he said.

"No." He looked puzzled.

"Thee is disappointed."

"Not really." I wanted to hit something. "My name is Martha—M-a-r-t-h-a!" My aim was true. He looked stricken.

"My speech offends thee."

"No, it's not that."

"Jer is disappointed about this afternoon."

He was belaboring the obvious. Then I looked at him, and saw him, scapegoat extraordinary, boy-believer in the holy family of us, surrogate

Ma and Pa Whitney, sometime common-law marrieds, at best. Why was I impatient with this dear, dopey, trusting boy with his nice face and body that weren't doing anyone a bit of good, least of all himself? How could he stand it—so young and all? Did he masturbate like crazy when we weren't around? Was he a closet gay? Or was he a eunuch-slave of God? Like those castrati Roman choirboys who used to sing in the Middle Ages?

"I think that's poison ivy." John was pointing to some shiny leaves in our path. I knew what was happening to me. The Jeremiah infection. Wandering eye to match the wandering foot. No, it wasn't that either. "Someone to Watch Over Me." Yes, music said it best. John would watch, surely, but no hands on her anywhere, no sirree. I'd have liked his hands, preferably with Jeremiah peering out the van window. Sinner! My head full of trash.

"You're smart about plants." I rose. "Let's go down to the Cave."

John took my hand, helping me up. Then he bent quickly, lifting my fingers to his lips. He kissed those fingers a long, slow time, not letting go, not looking at me. I felt shocked. So sudden, so sensual a gesture. It slid right under my clothes, as if he were kissing my pubis, putting his face right on it. Yet there we were, in this sort of formal stance right out of the eighteenth century. I could have been wearing a long, muslin dress—a Quaker dress!—and bonnet, too. He was wearing his usual black denims and black suspenders, and I imagined a black vest covering his narrow chest. I thought of the severe garb of the Amish, without the hat.

"I love thee," he murmured at my hand. "I know thee belongs to Jer, for sure, so don't be mad at me."

Poor Mealy-Mouth, I thought, the Devil working in me again, Jeremiah's personal devil beamed directly from the van. "Of course I'm not mad," I said, carefully withdrawing my hand. "But I don't belong to Jeremiah. Or anybody. I belong to me. And to God," I added, setting the record straight.

John was confused. He smiled helplessly. And then all the words and their meanings settled in. He looked at me hard. I'd have to be on my guard with him in the future.

We continued down the hill. He stepped lightly, like a scout on the trail, then stopped abruptly. With his watery blue eyes a little bulgy and scared he turned, finger on lips and signaled me to stop. I saw two men at the Cave entrance struggling with a uniformed man, apparently the guard.

The tall man had a shotgun, the short one a revolver. The guard was on the ground, kicking and shouting in the confused scuffle. A gun went off. The man cried and screamed, holding his shoulder. The shorter man lowered his revolver to the guard's temple and fired.

I may have screamed. John grabbed me hard and put his hand over my mouth till it hurt. He pulled me back from the scene. We were running, running over the leaves like deer back to the van. To Jeremiah! He was standing by the bench, agitated, holding his radio.

"They murdered the guard down there!"

"We're at war!" he countered.

His words didn't make sense. "Should we call the police?" John persisted.

"Police? Don't you understand what I'm saying? Our West Coast is bombed. We're under nuclear attack. We can be blown up right here!"

John quickly sorted out the news. "It's what you've been preaching, Jer. The end of the world!"

"What are you talking about?"

"John's right," I said. "Your forecast is coming true!"

" 'Forecast?' 'Forecast?' I wasn't talking about nuclear war, dummy. I was talking about sin!"

Dummy! It was too much. "The only dumb thing about me is that I believe in you! You wouldn't recognize sin if the Devil stuck his pitchfork in your ass!"

Jeremiah grabbed my shoulders.

"Fine! The world is coming apart and all you can do is get personal."

I began to laugh. It started with an itch, my whole body itched and it was funny. My body was laughing, throwing a fit to get rid of the itch, of Jeremiah, the shooting, the war, even John and our traveling circus of a God show.

Jeremiah slapped me. I began to cry. He put his arms around me and for a moment I felt limp.

"I'm sorry, Martha," he said. "We can't just stay here. We could be fried alive."

"The van—" said John.

"An incinerator. Nothing aboveground is safe. California's probably wiped out already."

"Why?" said John. "What's the war about?"

"Who knows? Somebody tripped over an island and bombs went off. What difference does it make now?" He flicked on the radio. We heard only static.

"Thee is right, Jer. Should we start digging, or something?"

"Digging?"

"You said nothing aboveground—"

"Oh, God!" groaned Jeremiah, in the manner of Job.

John flinched. "I know," he recovered. "The Cave." He pointed down the hill. To the murder scene.

Repelled, I recognized expediency and kept quiet.

"It has a big metal door."

"Lead?" asked Jeremiah wryly.

"It looks heavy."

"There's a stream inside," I said. "I heard people talking. It never made it as a tourist spot. They closed it up awhile back."

"Good," said Jeremiah. "Just the place."

"Suppose someone's there?"

"We'll have to take our chances."

"Suppose—there's a body at the entrance?"

"Stop creating obstacles!"

"Maybe somebody called the police and they took it away," John remarked.

"The police are all down in their cellars like everybody else, down on their everlasting knees! Let's get going before somebody else gets the idea and we have to stand in line."

We followed Jeremiah into the van, packed helter-skelter, threw food and blankets into a shopping cart, and emerged. Our leader threw out his arms to the sky. "Oh, Heavenly Father, show thy children the way!"

"Amen," John and I repeated, as we followed downhill.

In the clearing before the Cave entrance, we noticed the trail of blood. There was a big red splotch near the doors, a thin track into the bushes.

"He must be dead," I murmured. "They killed him here."

Jeremiah crossed himself as he stepped around the spot to the double doors. They were recessed beneath jagged boulders attesting to strength and sanctuary. The metal looked like steel, with large brass doorknobs. Jeremiah hesitated, glancing back at me.

"Hurry!" I said.

He pulled one knob, John pulled the other. The men struggled with the knobs. They threw themselves against the doors that rattled slightly. Those doors were locked.

"Get away from there! rasped a voice from the bushes. "What the hell do you think you're doing?"

I was frightened. "It's them."

five   **Entry**

"Get the fuck away from there!" Burns added his warning to Duke's as both men stepped out from the bushes. The blood trail lay between them and the trio like a scar. Burns carried a gun. Duke cocked his rifle.

"Don't shoot!" said Jeremiah. "We're not armed."

"Say," said Burns, still pointing his gun, "aren't you Jerry with the two flunkeys? Sure, Duke, look at them. Whaddya know."

"Aren't you the preacher?" called Duke.

"Yes—I'm a man of God. A man of peace. For God's sake put those guns down!"

"Trying to take over, eh, preach? Every man for himself? Where's that Christian charity you're spouting?"

"We thought—well, it is public property!" Jeremiah blurted.

"Sure," sneered Duke. "You'd take it over and keep the door open to the public, right?"

"Well—"

"Let everybody in, right, Preach?"

"I—"

"Like hell, you would. Now scram!"

Martha trembled. "Where's the guard?" she managed.

The two men turned on her. "What guard? What guard?" they shouted.

What had she said? "There's supposed to be a guard here," she responded weakly.

"Must be on vacation," said Burns.

"A lot of blood here," said John stubbornly.

"Come on, John!" urged Jeremiah.

"I shot a squirrel," said Duke.

"Weren't no squirrel," John insisted.

"Oh, come on!" pleaded Jeremiah, pulling his arm.

"Then it was a pig," said Duke. "Want to see?"

"Let's get out of here!" shouted Martha. She grabbed the handle of the cart.

"Just leave that, lady."

She looked at the shorter man. "What?"

"You heard me. You got a problem?"

"It's all the food we've got."

"My heart is breaking."

Suddenly they were not alone. A group of people came rushing noisily down the path on the far side of the Cave. Laden with boxes, suitcases, bedding, they formed a caravan of five, with Con in the lead. "What's up?" he called out.

"Nothing much," Duke answered. "Keeping the wolves from the door."

Mary was distraught. "Did you see Maybelle and Roy? They didn't get home. I should go back. Why did I come here?" she wailed. Abby tried to comfort her while Flora marched ahead.

"Who are these people?" asked Con. "Aren't they—"

"The preacher and company," said Duke. "They were just leaving."

"We want our food!" Martha told Con. "They're stealing our food!"

"We don't need your food," he assured her. He suddenly noticed the ground and asked, "Say, what happened here?"

"Nothing," said Duke. "I shot a skunk."

"It was a man—the guard!" Martha persisted. "And now they're taking our food and things. That cart is ours!"

"Look folks," Duke announced, "I have the key to the Cave." He raised the key. "We're wasting time. Guns and rifles are up in the car. We need to get them down here fast. Make up your minds. These damn troublemakers have got to go. You can let me take charge or stay outside and debate. It's up to you."

Flora approached Martha. "We don't want your food." She grabbed the shopping cart and thrust it toward the woman. "Go!" she ordered.

Martha took the cart.

"Great," said Burns. "All chiefs and no Indians. These bums are lucky to be alive and you're playing Santa Claus."

"Let's just move along," said Con.

"Hurry up, everybody!" urged Charles.

Abby echoed, "Hurry, hurry!"

Jeremiah, John, and Martha scurried back up the hill in full retreat.

"You've got guts," Burns muttered to Flora. She was a cool one.

Soon they'd all have guns, she thought. A stranger had probably died there. The guard? If so, in a sense he had died for them. Yet their only concern was shelter. Something wrong about all this. It was a new idea.

Duke motioned Charles to accompany him. He handed the key to Burns, who opened the door.

It was dark inside. Cool and damp. A dehumidifier would have been just the thing, mused Flora, glad of the sweater in her suitcase. But despite its gloomy interior, the Cave bespoke strength and sanctuary, their greatest need right now. There was a path of about forty feet, sloping down to a level of limestone, covered with patches of sand. A stream issued from beneath the entrance and flowed into the darkness, creating a pool deep within the Cave and dividing its floor in half. The right side was raised and formed a sort of ledge that dropped several feet near the wall. The left was irregular and zigzagged toward the interior. The ceiling was merely a canopy of rock, known to be shallow, and rested beneath a rise shaded by deep-rooted oaks. There were no stalagmites or stalactites or strange crystal or rock formations that might have sustained tourist interest. Even the town eventually gave up on the idea. It remained the destination for class trips by elementary school children, and then even those visits ceased. Maintenance fell to budget cuts until recently, when the Cave was closed.

The group started to transport their things. Charles and Duke went up the hill to Duke's car. Flora, Con, Abby, and Mary continued carrying supplies into the Cave. Burns kept watch, his gun tucked in his belt.

six   **Roy**

 We went to the Nature Trail because that was Maybelle's fa-
vorite place. She always liked to walk there. She liked to walk
period, since she'd been born with a slight leg deformity and
had plenty of physical therapy and a leg brace as a child. One of her legs
was a little bit thinner than the other, not much but enough to make us remember so we'd look at her as a little fragile though she wasn't.

Maybelle and I were close, not like Mary, our Mom, and her sister
Flora. They didn't get along. So when Dad left us, when he cut out and
ditched our whole scene, Mom got almost religious about me and Maybelle and us truly being friends. She'd say the best thing on earth was to
have a sibling you could trust. She talked about dying and how she wanted
us to have each other to turn to when she was gone. I think she always
wanted a brother, and then she got stuck with Aunt Flora, who was nice
and all but she and Mom were on different tracks, or maybe the same track
but coming from opposite directions so every once in awhile, boom! A
derailment.

It was hard for Mom. She worked part-time selling real estate, but that
wasn't much of a living. Grandpa Charles helped her, and he was great
about guaranteeing our education, so he eased the pressure about that. I
think what Mom really wanted was to have a husband the way Aunt Flora
did, a husband like Uncle Con, who was dependable and a real fun guy.
He took Maybelle and me fishing. Aunt Flora usually had something else
to do and besides she hated fishing. Uncle Con knew a lot about animals
and plants. He was great to have along on a hike. I think he would have
been a terrific biologist—he had so many good books on the subject. Instead he worked for an insurance company. He sort of didn't fit into what
he was doing, but he was the kind of guy who'd make the best of it. An easy
guy. Aunt Flora was kind of tense. A grown woman and she bit her nails.

140

She was very smart but I don't think she was happy. Uncle Con would pick up stray animals, an injured cat or bird or something, and it'd be there for a time, convalescing, and then it was gone. His wife didn't like to keep them around. She didn't even like the tropical fish. Maybe she just didn't like Uncle Con that much and couldn't come right out and say so.

We were on the trail with Jack and his sister Julia. Jack was my friend, kind of spoiled and wild but a real honest kid. Handsome too. We'd do anything for each other. I loved him but I was in love with Julia, in love since high school, and now we were both going away to college. Different colleges. A pain to think about but we had to face it. Her parents liked me well enough but they wanted Julia to go to a fancy school in Massachusetts. I couldn't afford to go out of town. My grades weren't good enough for a scholarship. It was expensive enough for Grandpa Charles to send me to the college nearby where I could drive to school. Julia's parents said that wasn't a good enough school for her implying it was good enough for the likes of me. I couldn't bear separation from Julia. It wasn't that she was so pretty, though she had nice features and wavy brown hair and a great smile, but the way she was sweet and strong at the same time made her downright beautiful—the most beautiful girl I ever saw.

The three-acre tract of the Nature Trail was a gift to the town from a very old lady whose people were some of the original settlers. There was a big, unclipped privet hedge that marked the limits of the Trail. The woman's house lay behind the hedge. You could see the four-story white frame with its gables that looked over the bushes. You knew the lady was there, and you wondered whether she was looking out from behind the draperies. Nobody saw her. They said she never went out.

Maybelle loved that house. She was kind of romantic and lived in her head a lot. I guess she made up stories about the place. The four of us stood there by the horse chestnut tree, looking up, and Maybelle said, "Maybe I like it because it's old, because it won't disappear when the weather changes." She was sort of talking about our Dad.

"Want to sit here, Maybelle?" Jack liked my sister. I felt a little sorry for him—he wasn't exactly her type. She was shy with guys. She'd get a secret crush on a teacher, an older man. Or she'd go for the poetic kind that looked as if they needed a nurse and a square meal and could recite "Ode on a Grecian Urn" or something. Not Jack. He worked out and played basketball until it took too much training and interfered with his social life. Even so, at heart Jack was a jock. Though I wasn't, I felt easier with him than anybody.

Julia and I left them and walked on ahead. We needed to talk. We spent a lot of time and energy avoiding the subject but summer was going fast. We walked past the small pond with its ducks and tiger lilies, the high banks of honeysuckle that sweetened the air. At the end of the Trail we sat down by the privet. Suddenly I didn't have the faintest idea of what to say. Jack had given me a joint camouflaged in a pack of cigarettes, which he didn't smoke.

"Share a smoke?" I asked, showing it to Julia.

"Out here?"

She was right. "Maybe not."

"I thought you didn't smoke anything."

"Jack gave it to me."

"Oh, Jack." Julia didn't approve a whole lot of what Jack did. She worried about him. He did pills too, sometimes. Their parents traveled a lot. Now they were away on some remote Greek island. Jack seemed to need attention. He'd cut up at parties. Once he went home so stoned we took him to a hospital. I stayed with him in Emergency. That was the worst time. Usually he was OK.

"So, you're really going away." It came out blunt. I didn't know how else to begin.

"I won't be in prison. I'll be back for holidays." She was playing it cool.

"Sure."

"Look, it wasn't my idea, though maybe it's a good one."

What could I say?

"Mother and Dad think we're too serious," she went on.

"Too young to know and all that crap."

"We *are* too young."

"And I don't have a hyphenated name." I was pushing.

"I don't, either!"

"You know what I mean."

"Please stop badmouthing my parents. They're not the snobs you think they are."

"I have a right to my opinion."

"What can I do?"

I didn't want her to cry, but I couldn't stop.

"What do you want to do?" I insisted.

"You know I prefer to stay—"

"Why not go to college right here? With me?"

"I'll feel the same about you wherever I am!"

"You won't give up anything. Some romantic dame."

She was getting angry. "What would you give up, Romeo? Tell me."

"I'd go to Massachusetts. Get a job near your school." I was thinking aloud, but I meant it.

"You'd give up school?"

"I could work my way through."

Julia was quiet. I would have done anything to stay with her. I don't know how many times in your life you can love like that. It wasn't puppyshit love. She used to do modern dance and sometimes she'd strain her back, and I'd get Bengay or something and rub her back gently, all over. I loved to carry her books, help her with math. She made me feel good about myself, like I was a real man and not just somebody's kid in school.

I saw the tears in her eyes. "You're crazy." I kissed her. We kissed a long time.

"I'm going to talk to them," she said. "They'll be back next week."

Julia wanted to stay. At least I had that.

"Shall we go to my house?" she said.

"My Mom expects us home for dinner." What a bummer. "You can come."

"I don't like barging in."

"Mom's not like that."

"Jack and I will get a pizza. He's busy later."

"Fine. I'll be over after dinner."

"We could go to the movies."

"Let's play it by ear." We were both smiling.

"Ro-oy!"

Maybelle being discreet, warning she was on the way. Jack and Julia would drop us off.

We piled into Jack's jeep. We turned toward Main Street and nearly hit a deer. A mother followed by two fauns leaped across the road. I'd never seen any this close to town, even though it was the Nature Trail area. Ducks and swans and rodent types, but no deer. Jack liked to drive fast. I told him to take it easy. He was pissed that the radio wasn't working. He wanted some gas, but the station seemed deserted. He honked his horn. No one appeared. "It's not a holiday or anything." The rest of us were puzzled. "Damn," he said, "I'm a little low but we'll make it."

Our house lay at the edge of town. We drove down Main Street then turned.

There wasn't any traffic. It was eerie. Air not stirring, Dutch elms just standing there like they couldn't care less.

The shops were closed! On Saturday. No traffic. Nobody walking around. I remembered the W. C. Fields joke about Philadelphia on Sunday and thought, Went to Main Street on Saturday. It was closed. The supermarket really scared us. The big, bustling, nearly-always-open supermarket—closed!

Jack zoomed down the empty lane. We reached the mailbox that read "Williams" and turned into the driveway. Mom's car was gone. I jumped out. The Post-It on the screen door read: "See note on kitchen table." I unlocked the door and we went in.

You could tell someone had been rushing around—cabinet doors open, drawers pulled out, a couple of towels on the kitchen table. I read the note.

"Dear Roy and Maybelle: Nuclear war started. West Coast bombed.

Come immediately to the Cave. All arranged. I packed for you. Love, Mom."

Do not pass "Go" I thought wildly. Go directly to Cave. I tried calling Mom's cell phone. Mine wasn't working. Our land line seemed dead. We turned on the radio: static. The TV—just channel numbers. I unplugged it—our customary fire safety measure. Mom always used to unplug the set when we went away. She sure had left in a hurry.

The refrigerator was nearly empty. The cupboard was pretty bare. "There's a jar of artichoke hearts!" exclaimed Maybelle.

"We've got to get out of here."

But we all were hungry. We quickly shared half a container of milk, some whole wheat bread, and the artichoke hearts—Mom liked them for parties I thought grimly. A fast, loony farewell to civilization. We picked up a few extra clothes for Jack and Julia, used the bathrooms, and cleared out. We did all this in about five minutes. Maybelle had something in a bag. I guessed it was her Teddy bear. I thought of taking my stamp collection, but that was silly. We wouldn't be away that long. And we sure as heck couldn't live forever in a cave.

"You and Jack can borrow our clothes," Maybelle told Julia.

"Do you think it's OK? We're not invited—" Julia remarked as we rushed to the jeep.

"This isn't a freaking dinner party!" I checked my irritation. "We're all going. Period."

I glanced back at the maple tree in the yard where the swing used to be, the mound of leaves on the right where little Maybelle and Roy used to build their fort in the winter. By the road was the rock garden that Mom had had so much trouble with, every year trying new plants, perennials that rarely survived. I saw the santolina, gray-green and green that she finally triumphed with, and remembered her delight with its yellow and white flowers in the spring. And there was our house, the house we'd grown up in, real plain with a front porch, cedar shingle, two stories with a storage attic, a little brown house as a neighbor had uncharitably put it to Mom who had expected it to turn gray from weathering and wanted to sock the woman, but smiled. I noted the white trim Maybelle and I had painted in that orderly other life last year. It was like looking at a movie screen getting tinier in the distance. Your whole life disappearing into your head.

"Maybe we should pass by our house. Pick up some stuff. I wish we could reach our folks," Jack mumbled, "wherever the heck they are." He wasn't getting it.

"You can check back at your house later." I knew that wouldn't happen, but there was no time for detours.

"I'm low on gas."

"For God's sake, let's get to the Cave! It's not far. We'll figure it out from there."

Julia took my hand. We sat behind Jack and Maybelle, bumping along in the open jeep.

"What do you think it's all about?" said Jack.

"Damned if I know. Tit for tat. Power politics." I thought of Maybelle sitting up front with her Teddy bear. I thought of the little kids on the West Coast, like the kids in Vietnam years ago, screaming and holding on to their burning dolls or whatever, kids with their hair on fire and skin crackling and eyes boiling in their sockets, naked and screaming for their mothers and fathers. I'd read about Hiroshima and Nagasaki crumbled to ash and generations of suffering. I imagined radioactive rubble in San Francisco and Los Angeles, crashing skyscrapers and mansions with swimming pools and tennis courts and schools and slums and orange groves and factories and giant computers crushing everybody to death and all the students sitting there crammed with lessons they'd just learned, all the music and show tunes and movie sets, planes falling out of the sky and breaking into thousands of smoky piles and pieces of bodies everything with a funny glow contaminated untouchable open-air crematoria turning everybody and everything into junk into permanently radioactive junk. I squeezed Julia's hand and tried to look brave.

"I'm scared," she whimpered. I kept up the role. "It'll be OK." We were on the way to a hole in the ground. Manhood equals molehood. Moles were lucky! They already had their tunnels.

Maybelle crouched down real small. Jack was mumbling, "Who needs this! Who needs their dirty war!"

He was right. I just wanted to be with Julia and go to school. I wanted to go home and stay in bed for a week. I didn't want to turn on. Just drop out of their goddamn wars and shit. One two three four, we don't need your dirty war.

We were at the turn. The Cave was way down, like the Town dump. Except that it didn't smell. Not yet, anyway. We pulled up next to Mom's convertible. I saw my grandfather's Chrysler, Flora and Con's SUV. I didn't recognize the brown car.

We ran down the path to the big gray doors. I remember Mom taking us there as kids. I hadn't seen them in years. Nobody went there anymore. I think they kept a guard just to avoid lawsuits. Nothing to see. Just a hole with rocks. Nobody was around.

"Ma!" we yelled and banged on the doors. "Open up. It's Roy and Maybelle."

The left door opened a crack. It was Mom. "Oh, thank God you're here! Come in. We were all so worried." I knew that Mom had worried enough for everyone.

"Jack and Julia are with us."

"All right, all right. Come on!"

Behind her a voice rumbled, "Hold on there. What do you think you're doing?"

A tall man came over. I could barely make out his face in the dim light. I'd seen him once at Aunt Flora's. He was carrying a rifle.

"Come in," said my mother, real firm.

"Only your kids," he warned her.

"Come in!"

Jack and Julia hung back. We all did. We were intimidated by the rifle. I held Julia's hand. "There are four of us!" I said real loud.

"Two," said the tall man. "I'm closing the door. We've got to keep the air clean in here. There's no more room."

"Yes, there is!" shouted my mother.

"The two of you—in or out."

Mom dashed outside. She grabbed Maybelle who was screaming. Con tried to pull me inside. I wrenched free. Julia was yelling for me to go in while her brother stood helplessly.

"This is a countdown. Ten—nine—eight—"

I hated that crazy bastard.

"Seven—six—five—"

I saw Aunt Flora's face and Grandma Abby and Grandpa Charles— faces looking scared and small, faces I might never see again. Mom still clutched Maybelle's hand.

"Roy!" she kept shouting. "Please come in!"

"Four—three—"

I gave my sister a push through the door and it clanged shut.

Suddenly I was frightened, wanting to change my mind and beg them to let me in, running to my mother, leaving Jack and Julia flat, saving myself. I didn't want to be some stupid hero. And I didn't want to cry either— not in front of Jack and Julia. I pounded the door till my fist hurt and shouted till I was hoarse. Muffled voices were arguing inside. Julia looked at me funny.

"It's my fault," she said.

"Shut up!"

And then I started to get mad, really mad at the pack of them in there. Safe. My family abandoning me! That guy with the rifle. Were they prisoners? Outside I might be fried with my two best friends. Some comfort. I tried to be glad for Maybelle.

Jack had gone scouting a little ways. "Hey, there's a van up there. We ought to get under cover."

"Above ground is no cover."

"Better than nothing. We can't drive anywhere." Jack's tone changed. "We ought to slash that guy's tires!"

"I'll check out the cars," I said.

I left the two of them and took off. I didn't have my own key to Mom's car. Still a child! Little Roy! A man would've had his own key. Where could we go? The other cars were locked and empty. Jack was right. What I really wanted to do was slash the guy's tires. Get some payback.

I had my Swiss Army knife. I would stab the tires of the brown car. I picked up a rock. I'd smash the windshield! I was going to declare war too! But on whom? Was it the right car? Did it matter? My own country hadn't even declared war. They didn't feel the need to. That was playing by old rules that no one paid attention to anymore. It was like planes dropping bombs ignoring who was being hit. Just find the anonymous target. No blood. Coordinates on a screen. Like a computer game. Yeah. That was the new kind of war. Cool!

Julia and Jack were calling me. I went back down. We followed Jack up the other side of the hill and headed for the van. He rushed ahead then stumbled and sat down. Klutz! He had sprained his ankle.

"Lean on me." I helped him the rest of the way. He was apologetic. I thought Jack fell down and broke his crown and Julia came tumbling after. How I ached to be in the Cave! If only Julia had been with me. Or Maybelle. Maybe if we'd had Jack and Julia follow us later—much later, ha!— I'd be safe in the Cave. With my family. Maybe, holy Maybe!

"Jeez, I'm a drag," said Jack. "If we can get into that van, I'll stay and you can try going back to the Cave with Julia."

"You're nuts."

"It's a good idea."

"It's lousy. I'd need a gun to go back there."

He looked glum. Guess he was feeling guilty.

"You should go back, Roy," Julia told me.

"Didn't you hear what I said to your brother?" I wasn't in the mood to give reassurance. I had hardly enough for myself.

The van was blue with little blinds all around. It was the preacher's. You couldn't even see into the rear windows. Heavenly blue we had joked when we saw it in town.

We banged on the door and a woman came to the window. She peeked through the blinds.

"What you want?"

"Please let us in." She disappeared. Again I knocked on the door.

"We need shelter. Please. We can't go anyplace. My friend sprained his ankle."

She reappeared at the window. "No room in here."

I got mad again and now I felt like throwing a rock at *her* window. She wouldn't even open the door. I punched it.

"My family—they've prisoners in the Cave. A guy with a rifle won't let us in and now you won't either. What kind of God are you preaching?"

The woman vanished. Julia looked as if she was going to bawl. I wanted to but I started looking for rocks. If the whole world was locking us out I'd fight back. Then all of the sudden the door opens and this tall skinny guy says, "Come in." It was the preacher.

seven   **Mary**

I felt like Solomon with the baby they were going to divide in half to settle a dispute except that nobody asked me and they did cut up my child, half outside the Cave, half inside. I guess I carried on screaming and crying, well what was I supposed to do with my baby Roy outside? How could you be a fifty percent winner in a situation like that? OK, there was no situation like that except maybe in concentration camps. Like in *Sophie's Choice*, where the Nazi commander made the woman pick one of her two children to save — except that I hadn't chosen. And we were all neighbors! We could have been a crowd of gorillas. No, I saw gorillas in the movies and public television. They lived peaceably in families. Families! Maybe we had the wrong ancestors. Maybe *Pithecanthropus erectus* was a creep. I felt split right down the middle. I had my Maybelle, but that made it hurt even more.

Abby mothered me. She stopped feeling sorry for herself and put her arms around me and cried with me. It helps to have someone to cry to, to cry with. My father was busy gnashing his teeth. Con would have held me, you just know those things. But Flora would have had a fit. Not screamy like me but a lip-biting, spitting-eyed one. I couldn't blame her, though she was the original dog in the manger about Con. She really didn't want him though she sure didn't want me to have him. According to Flora, I'd had the cream. A husband *and* kids. Husband! He seared my wounds with alcohol. He didn't even try to stop drinking. I think he went away so he could kill himself in private, nobody nagging him about it. I did have the kids. So their uncle came over occasionally. Why not? That was natural. He never made a pass at me, I never made a pass at him. Sure, I thought about it, imagined what it would be like in bed with him. Flora wouldn't discuss her marriage with me — how's that for a younger sister? — but I gathered he was equipped OK. Maybe I could teach him a couple of things. I'd been on my own a while.

151

"You'd better open the door." Con looked fierce. Everybody looked fierce in that dim light from the butane lamp. We were saving the flash-light batteries. He sort of came right out of the rocks. I felt good that he was speaking up. Even Charles had protested.

"You may be the leader of this group, but you're not the dictator."

"That's downright unfriendly," said Duke.

"Go have an election," Burns muttered.

Con reached over and tried to open the door, but Burns stuck the gun in his back. It was awful. He ordered Con away from the door and Con kept insisting he put the weapon away. I was frantic.

And then I realized Duke had pulled Maybelle over to him. In my panic over Con I'd let go of her. Now Maybelle was crying and Duke was comforting her!

"Look folks," Duke said calmly, "Roy made his own choice. He's not a baby. He'll find a way to survive. People do. We can't overcrowd the prem-ises or strain our supplies. We might be here a long time. I suggest we set-tle in and relax. What we all need is a drink."

"Put your guns away first," said Con. "Both of you."

"No sweat," said Duke, "when the atmosphere gets a bit cozier. Let's work on it."

I was frozen. He was still holding on to Maybelle and started walking off with her, deeper into the Cave.

"You come back here, Maybelle!"

Duke turned on me.

"Listen, lady, Burns and I may get a mind to throw you all out of here. We teamed up nice and friendly, neighbors helping each other out. You need good company in hard times, right? Who knows how long we'll have to stay here. Maybe we'll come out and we'll be the only ones around and have to start a new town, like Noah without the animals and a lot worse off. Soon everything may be dead or radioactive or both. We need to work together. So let's get with the program. Anybody want a drink from this bottle"—he raised a quart of scotch from his shoulder bag and set it down at his feet—"just help yourselves."

Burns rushed over to the peace offering. He raised the bottle to his lips and drank a few gulps. "Come on," he invited. "Hey, Flora—come on over. You played hostess. Now it's our turn," he chuckled.

She wouldn't move. "Didn't think you were a party pooper," he coaxed. "It's medicine—a nerve tonic. No takers? The hell with everybody. I'm getting settled."

At Duke's insistence we camped on both sides of the stream: he, Burns, and Maybelle on the right, with the guns. The rest of us—Con, Flora, my parents, and me on the left. We had most of the supplies. Duke had several rifles. He was armed with two guns in his belt. Burns had one. Duke started walking away with Maybelle. I knew she was scared to death.

I went crazy again, screaming at him. I wanted to gouge out his eyes. I wanted to kill him. He was kidnapping my child and nobody was stopping him. At the same time I had a wild urge to run out to Roy. I hated everybody.

Flora slapped me. "Shut up! Shut up!" she kept saying.

"What do you care?" I blurted out. "You don't have any children."

Her eyes were all yellow in that light, a cat's eyes. We stared at each other over years of Abby's favoring me, of competing for grades and boyfriends, over years of plain dislike. Sometimes I think it's chemical, the way people interact. Sometimes I think Flora and I developed allergies to each other.

"You *are* a bitch," she said. I hadn't wanted to hurt her that much. Abby was getting very upset. Flora backed down because there was an audience and she had some feeling about my situation with the kids. Con shut us both up. He drew us aside and whispered, "We need a gun." So the crying session turned into a conference. It calmed me a little.

He was right. We had no weapons. Knives, but nothing sharp enough. Nothing powerful as a gun. We needed to get one away from either of them. Duke was too well-armed, too formidable. Burns was the chosen target.

"He seems to like you," I told my sister. "Maybe you could get his gun away from him." Why had I said that? It was a good idea—I still believe— but I wish Flora had thought of it first. Or even Con.

She looked at me in a way I won't forget.

"I'll take care of it," Con announced quietly in his let-big-brother-do-it fashion.

Flora was firm. "He'll be on guard with you. I can do it. Let me try." Con couldn't deter her. The more he argued the more determined she got.

I couldn't stand her looking at me. Accusingly. I wanted to say forget it, but the words got stuck. If it had been Victorian times I could have conveniently fainted. But I wanted to get out of there by any means necessary. With Maybelle. And find Roy. Leave the Cave, that crazy rear march to the Stone Age.

We started to settle into the half-light, our half-life, our nightmare. It might be over in the morning. Soon be over, soon be over, the kids used to sing. "All My Trials, Lord." Was I supposed to thank Flora for her grand gesture, suggested by me? Maybe she'd change her mind. Part of me hoped she would.

The rest of me didn't.

eight   John

When thee believes in something, believe all the way or else it won't work. God knows what you're about, he can see right through to the back of thy head. Thee has to pray hard so nothing gets stuck, so God's heavenly vacuum cleaner can reach in and suck out all the unclean thoughts. I wanted Martha. We took that little walk and I wanted her. It was wrong. How could I confess such a thing to Jeremiah? To her? They weren't that old but they were my family, like my mother and father. I didn't have to think of them that way. Maybe I just wanted to maybe it was safer so I wouldn't keep getting mixed up. I knew what was going on, how she loved him and he fooled around in every town we stayed at more than ten minutes. That's not so but you get the idea. He needed to relax his own way. I knew the situation. I weren't that dumb. She kept loving him and loving him and not getting loved back the way she wanted. I could have told her Jeremiah was special, more than we could figure out. But then I'd be thinking Martha was special too, so I didn't say anything. Besides, we knew that God was telling him things.

God tapped Jeremiah on the shoulder saying do this do that. About the women — God must have a reason for that too. He was full of good reasons we couldn't begin to understand. Faith helped us but even faith couldn't go all the way. Only God knows about that. And He doesn't need to explain.

Martha was a practical woman. She knew we didn't have much food and stuff in the van. Though she was protecting us I was real proud of Jeremiah. The way he said, Step right in, like the Lord was going to set the table for them. Three kids: Roy, Jack, Julia. Jack had the bum ankle. Julia looked kind of sickly. Maybe she was just scared. We were all scared. Roy seemed the most together. At least he didn't complain out loud about anything.

Jeremiah took charge. Everybody sat down, sort of squeezed together, but Jer was figuring the next step. He asked the strangers about themselves and they told us about the Cave. Martha let them know what we'd seen there. She said it seemed like a good place to hide. The three of them agreed.

"You can't hide," said Jeremiah, as if forgetting he'd ever been interested in the Cave. "You can't hide from God's vengeance if he's showing it." Jer sounded strange. He got a bottle of wine from the food cabinet. "Are you Christians?" he asked the visitors.

"Why?" Roy looked surprised.

"I thought we'd have a communion—before leaving. You don't have to be anything special if you want to take part."

Martha stared at him. I guess she didn't like his using up the wine like he was showing off in front of visitors, especially the girl. And communion was something private we shared on special holidays. Well this was a special time for sure. Martha looked at Jer the way you'd look at a skinny Santa Claus with his black hair hanging out. She didn't say nothing just got out our three cups and three glasses. We had only a little bread left. So she passes around some pretzels. Sort of funny like it was supposed to be a party but it wasn't.

Jer stood up and raised his cup. "Thanks be to God for blessings received. Protect us in this day from the wrath of Thy judgment." It wasn't exactly what he usually said at communion and I didn't get the wrath part unless he meant the war. I knew he was being friendly and trying to make us all feel better. We raised our drinks like a toast. I didn't know what the heck it was.

Roy set his glass down. "I'm thankful you took us in, sir. But this is a terrible situation." He sounded like a skeptic.

"I wish we could open a window," said Martha.

"Better not," Jeremiah warned. "There may be fallout."

"Fallout!" she says. "It could take years to kill you and if you're lucky you'll be dead by then anyway." She was getting edgy.

"Is there any more news?" the girl asked. "Our parents are on a Greek island . . . I think." She was almost about to cry.

Martha picks up the radio. Static, same as before. "How's your ankle?" she asks Jack.

"A little better."

She brings him a stool. "Put your foot up."

"Thanks."

Jeremiah didn't care for Roy's words. "You ought to be thankful you're alive."

"Yes, sir. But in a little while it might be lousy to be alive anywhere."

Martha spoke up. "The Cave should be safe." I was glad she could hang on to an idea.

"I'm thankful," Jer went on, "that I can share with my fellow humans the whiplash of misfortune." I liked the sound of that. It was his preaching voice. Then he picks up the usual theme. "Man is sinful. Pitiful as he is, he must suffer. It's the human condition—suffering and asking why why why. Prophets say, Repent! Nobody listens. Repent! Nobody listens. So God gets angry." He hesitated. "Maybe that's what's happening now," he finished sort of lamely, churning out the familiar words and suddenly running out of steam. He'd never said "maybe" before.

"Thee preaches salvation, too," I reminded, uncomfortable that I might be sort of correcting Jer, and in front of strangers.

"Without a doubt," he says. He looks kind of lost.

"Salvation of the everlasting soul," I timidly add.

"Amen."

"You think suffering is a good thing?" Roy asks Jeremiah.

"Not good or bad," Jer says, picking up steam. "It just is. It's from God and God can't be bad. So in that sense, it's good. Suffering is a lesson reminding us of our evils, our destructiveness."

"You mean like making war—a dumb, stupid war that nobody knows anything about—that nobody cares about even if they did know?" I watched Jer struggling.

"Wars are—a dramatization."

"A what?" asked Roy. Even I hadn't heard that one before.

"A dramatization of evil. Sin! The way people are."

"Say," Jack spoke up, "if people are rotten, why the hell—excuse me—

why do you want to save them? Maybe they—we—*should* all burn up. Then there won't be any more problems."

Jer was tiring of the discussion. I could tell the way he tensed up his neck muscles and stuck out his jaw.

"Salvation is a gift," he went on. "God so loved the world—"

"Tough love," says Roy.

"—that he gave his only begotten Son."

"So then he didn't think it was so bad."

"You have all the answers," Jer said.

"Sorry—what I meant was, what about the teachings—what Jesus said about loving people. Loving your neighbors—everybody. Man, I learned that in Sunday School! I thought *all* religions were about love and good deeds. What about turning the other cheek? And I thought you were supposed to *do* things, constructive things."

Jer was fed up. "Maybe *you* ought to take up preaching," he tells Roy.

"There are enough preachers around." The kid was getting sassy and I didn't like it. "Hold on there," I say.

"You're being rude!" says Martha.

"Sorry. I don't mean to sound disrespectful but I feel pretty crummy," the kid went on. "My mother and sister, my aunt and uncle and grandparents are down in that creepy Cave with a couple of crazy guys with guns. I'm scared of what's going on in there—they could all be dead! All because of this dumb crazyass rotten war! Jeez, I wouldn't want my child to grow up in a world like this. Who wants to have a radioactive monster baby?"

I wished Jeremiah hadn't let them in. What a bunch of negatives! Didn't have enough spirit to spark a dead battery. You open the door and let in trouble. Jer was too good for them. Weren't going to let anybody else in, that was for sure. I knew Martha was thinking the same thing. I couldn't always make out what Jer was thinking, but he'd probably go along with us on this. The way we felt.

nine   Vengeance

 It was dark outside the Cave. A station wagon pulled up behind the Chrysler. A disheveled woman jumped out. The driver, a stocky man carrying a rifle, followed her. "Stay there," he told the three men in the car. They, too, carried rifles.

The woman ran down the hill. "Harry! Harry!" she shouted. It was quiet all the way down through the stones and bushes. Only crickets and katydids and spare, ghostly trees marked her flight. A moon revealed the oval doors to the Cave, doors shut as firmly as the entrance to a mausoleum. The woman hit the door with her fists. "Harry! For God's sake— you in there?"

The stocky man said, "Come on, Trudy. He ain't there." He scanned the entrance with a flashlight, then aimed it at the ground. "Looks like something happened here. Something bad."

"What's that?"

"Not sure. Blood, maybe."

The woman started to shriek. "Won't do no good," the man said. "We'd better get out of here."

"We got to find him, Joe. We got to find my husband!" She began to wail.

"Now look, Trude, you got to quit that. Let's go back to the car and scout around a little. Come on, Trudy. I'm his brother, remember. And we got three other brothers in the car. Come on."

They got back into the car, joining the somber men. Joe reached into the glove compartment.

"What you doing?"

He put an object in her lap. "Now put this in your bag, kid. You know how to us it, right? Want me to show you again?"

She shook her head and dropped the gun into her purse.

"The safety catch is on and it's loaded. Mike, Bob, Tim," he addressed the others, "keep your eyes peeled. We gonna sniff around."

"Look at these cars here," said Mike. "I bet there's somebody in the Cave."

"Could be a lotta people in there," said Bob.

"Yeah," agreed Tim.

"Maybe," admitted Joe. "And we're gonna find out, right?" He gritted his teeth. "We'll come back."

He backed up the car, drove slowly around to the other side of the rise, and pulled up beside the van. "Say, looks like the preacher's van. Maybe he saw something." Joe honked the horn until the blind was half-raised and a woman's face appeared. A man's face looked out, then the blind was lowered.

"We better try harder," said Joe. "Insist on a little hospitality," he added grimly. "OK, Trude. Remember your purse. I'll leave my rifle. Don't want to scare anybody, but you never can tell. Better give me the gun for now, just in case." Trudy handed it to him and he slid it into his pants pocket. They went to the rear doors of the van and started banging.

"Please!" yelled Trudy. "I'm looking for my husband! Please help me!"

"Don't mean any harm!" Joe shouted.

When the door finally opened a crack, Joe pulled it the rest of the way and they climbed into the crowded space. A beanpole of a woman shut the door quickly behind the two strangers.

"What you want?" asked Martha.

Trudy gazed frantically past her to the three young people seated on one of the two benches flanking the interior, a kerosene lamp on a plastic-covered table behind them. Jeremiah and John rose from the other bench.

"The guard—the guard—" said Trudy, her voice breaking. It sounded like "the god—the god." Martha stared at the intruders.

"We're looking for my brother," Joe took over. "He's the security guard of the Cave. This here's his wife. You seen anybody with a uniform? Seen him down there at all?"

Trudy was weeping. "There's no place to sit," said Martha.

"Look, ma'am," Joe snapped, "we don't want no tea party."

"Well," Martha hesitated, "maybe we saw him."

"What you mean, 'maybe'?"

"Weren't no cop or no soldier," said John. "Must've been the guard."

"Where did he go?"

Martha and John remained silent. "My friends think they saw your husband," offered Jeremiah. "They don't want to upset you. They think he was hurt."

Joe turned suspicious. "What do you mean, 'hurt'?"

"Shot."

"I knew it was something bad!" moaned Trudy.

"There were two men—"

"Seemed like they were taking over the Cave," volunteered John.

"Everybody was fighting," said Martha. "A gun went off. They carried him away."

"And you just watched them?"

"We were scared. We're not armed."

"Where did they take him? Is he dead?"

"They dragged him someplace."

"God help me!"

"Come on now, Trude," Joe comforted. "We'll get them."

"Where did they take him?" the woman insisted.

"I don't know," said Martha. "Away from the Cave. To the right, as you face it. Into the trees."

"Behind the Cave—to the right?" asked Joe.

"Yes."

"Where'd they go?"

"I guess they're in the Cave."

"Now?"

"Seems so."

"OK," said Joe. "We got news for them. My three brothers and me. But first we got to find our brother. You better come with us." He motioned to Martha. She cringed.

"What for?"

"Show us where they took him."

"I told you!"

"Show us," he said evenly. "Want to make sure he's not in the Cave."

"He's not there!" said John.

"How you so sure, now?"

"Look, said Jeremiah, "they're telling you what they saw."

"You the preacher, huh?"

"I'm Jeremiah."

"Maybe you better come too. You may need to do a whole lot of praying."

"Wait a minute, brother," said Jeremiah.

"Got enough brothers, preacher."

"There's some other people in there," said Martha. "They have guns."

"How many people?" Joe asked skeptically.

"About seven, I guess."

"We're wasting time, lady."

"Better slow down," John cautioned.

"What'll you do if you get everybody out of there?" Martha asked.

"Go home to our families. Want to finish this business."

"Well," she put in quickly, "then maybe we could move into the Cave." She indicated the others in the van.

"Might come back and join you," said Joe, half-smiling.

Martha hesitated.

"Might not work out," he said abruptly. "Let's get going."

Roy stood up. "Those other people inside — they're my family!"

"Sure thing." Suddenly the man was holding a gun.

"What's that for?" Jeremiah asked in alarm.

"Insurance policy. All right. Everybody out."

"This is crazy! You don't need us. 'Vengeance is mine, saith the Lord.' "

"Come on, Buster," snarled Joe. Everyone followed him and Trudy out of the van.

"Maybe this time we'll all get in," remarked Roy.

"Yeah," quipped Jack. "A family reunion."

Roy took his arm. "How's the foot?"

"Fine." He winced. "Sort of."

"My brother has a sprained ankle!" Julia warned. No one paid attention.

Jeremiah was last. From the table he deftly retrieved the small Bible and slipped it into his trouser pocket with the loose change. Like a mantra he kept thinking, I am the Way, the Truth, and the Life, and turned off the lamp.

ten **In the Cave | Burns**

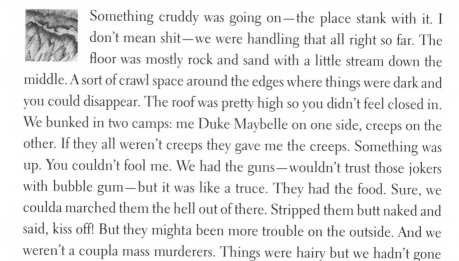Something cruddy was going on—the place stank with it. I don't mean shit—we were handling that all right so far. The floor was mostly rock and sand with a little stream down the middle. A sort of crawl space around the edges where things were dark and you could disappear. The roof was pretty high so you didn't feel closed in. We bunked in two camps: me Duke Maybelle on one side, creeps on the other. If they all weren't creeps they gave me the creeps. Something was up. You couldn't fool me. We had the guns—wouldn't trust those jokers with bubble gum—but it was like a truce. They had the food. Sure, we coulda marched them the hell out of there. Stripped them butt naked and said, kiss off! But they mighta been more trouble on the outside. And we weren't a coupla mass murderers. Things were hairy but we hadn't gone bonkers yet. We couldn't trust them—not in a pig's ass. Anyway we needed a little communication.

What a bonzo joint. The whole deal. To think I used to have some respect for these people like they were hot stuff living on the Heights and changed their fancy bedsheets every frigging week even though the jerkoffs didn't even know how to sweat! Here they were trying to take over like they were still running things. Smell the coffee! We were the ones giving protection. Duke with his arsenal and them quacking around like a gang of hysterical geese. So Duke could get a little out of line. Working too fast with that kid Maybelle. Never saw him so hot for pussy. Don't know what got into him—she wasn't that much of a looker though she was sure young enough and those boobs jiggling under her T-shirt. Shi-i-it! That wasn't smart her mother right there and all. Wasn't for me to be critical— hell he was my only friend in the place maybe in the world. He could act like he was a king or something sometimes. He could tell them all to fuck off he knew he could buy and sell the lot of them a dozen times over from here to next Tuesday. Maybe a hundred times. He coulda been one of them Swiss bank fellas with the numbered accounts they hid in cuckoo clocks or some shit. Duke was the kinda guy you didn't really know and him letting you think you did. A smart fella. You needed a boss in a stinking situation like this. Hell you always needed a boss to run things especially with a buncha yo-yos. Charles: dumb diddler with a Chrysler. Abby: a barrel of laughs going over Niagara Falls. Con: a Boy Scout. Mary: a loser. And Flora—I couldn't figure her. Well I could. She had hot pants she hadn't taken off lately except to pee. Something else got to me.

Couldn't figure it. Was it that crazy place—everything so dim? Their side lighter so we could watch them and be private at the same time? Was it her ladyship face looking superior—a pale narrow face thin hair pulled to the side with a girl's hair clip? Shirt a boy could wear narrow hands and feet like her body didn't have space to stretch out? Funny the things that attracted you. She wasn't what anybody would call sexy but she sure as hell turned me on.

When she walked over to me Duke was away back in the Cave with Maybelle. I felt myself getting a hard-on right then and there. Fuck! It's a good thing I was sitting down. I touched the gun in my belt just in case. I wasn't fooling myself that she was gonna pass the doughnuts and coffee but I felt good she was coming over just the same. The light on the other side was like watching TV. We were saving the batteries and fuel. Con had the fuel for his lamp kinda dim now. We'd had something to eat. Duke was playing a CD real low. He was a great one for gadgets. He liked hard rock and sweet dance music from the forties and knew people and setting up a romantic mood. I think he was playing "Old Black Magic" and remembered the kind of stuff Flora and Con played at their house only a few hours ago. Maybe Duke liked Flora too but was concentrating on the girl. What a joke if to her he was a dirty old man.

Duke was playing real soft and polite. I guess he was trying to loosen things up all around. I could see Maybelle's mother sitting bolt upright like a scarecrow with X-ray eyes beamed over at them. They had room to move over to the ledge where nobody could see them not even me. That Mary number was a trip. Couldn't blame her it was her daughter. I wished I coulda dumped the little broad over the stream into Mommy's aching lap.

I could feel trouble especially when it was coming my way. In my scalp my gut all over. I knew Duke was trouble and I knew Flora was trouble. But when you tingle like that some people turn tail and run. Me I just stand there taking it in. Hell it's interesting. You got plenty of time to be bored when you're laid out. Getting laid is something else. I'll snatch a little of that stuff thanks. But bored stiff be my guest. I don't dig it. Might as well dig a *grave*. Fuck that.

Didn't kid myself that Flora was coming to my everlasting charms or arms. I thought maybe she had a knife and was going to slip it to me right in the gut. Then I wondered. It was hard to see her face. She had her back to the light. "You a missionary or something?" I kidded just to see where her head was at.

"I'm on a peace mission." She was sort of smiling. I took off my jean jacket—it was cool in there—and put it beside me for her to sit with me on the rock. I was a regular Sir Galahad or Sir Lancelot I forget which. The one with the balls.

"You from the United Nations?" I was surprised she was sitting this close. I touched the piece in my belt again just in case. She caught that and said, "You afraid of me?" I laughed. She could get to me that one.

So she sat on my jacket and there was Benny Goodman easing out of the air. She was staring at me and suddenly I felt like an ape with these long hairy arms I wanted to grab her with. "Shall we dance?"

She laughed. Sure I was joking but she didn't have to laugh so hard like she was laughing at the idea of me more than the dancing. Maybe we were all in a fucking zoo but I wasn't one of the animals. I could have strangled her.

"What's up?"

She didn't answer right away. Kept sitting there close. She was asking for it. "Mary's pretty miserable."

"It's a tough life."

"You should have let her son in. And his friends—"

"Get off my back with that shit! It's yesterday. Next?"

"She's worried about Maybelle."

So that was it. "What the fuck do you want me to do?"

"Just—understand how she feels."

Flora was getting on my nerves. "Holy shit!" I think I scared her. She got quiet. Then she said, "Mary is a delicate person."

"What am I—a shrink or something? Go tell Sigmund Freud." I felt smug about that jab in her territory. It livened her up.

"Oh, you're really smart aren't you Mr. Burns."

"Yes, Ms. Prunewhip. Up yours." I wasn't taking any more crap. "You come over here like you're doing the natives a favor with your ass on my jacket. Get this straight: Duke's the boss here and you're lucky he doesn't throw the whole buncha you the fuck out. Maybe he ought to and be done with it. This is getting to be a pain in the butt. I think him and me ought to work it out once and for all."

She seemed scared. "I didn't mean—"

"C'mon what's the game?" I wouldn't let her back out. She got sort of small and hunched over. I had the advantage.

She didn't answer right away so I said like I was casually changing the subject, "How's your love life?" At any other time I woulda said, How's your sex life? But I didn't want to push too fast. She wasn't talking.

We were near the wall. I didn't think anyone could see us. Like I said she was a lady wearing a skirt the one she'd put on for dinner a thin cotton skirt that spread out like a flower. A skirt you could reach up into without ripping any seams a here-I-am-come-and-get-it kind of skirt. She was so thin and hairless I wondered whether she had any hair down there. I was still pretty hot but I don't think she noticed anything. It woulda done her good if she had. I was going to say something about Con then dropped it as the wrong tack. For a minute I didn't know what to say and just put my hand over hers gently as if a little snake was crawling over it cool and slow. "You have guts," I said. "I thought your Boy Scout woulda come over here himself." I couldn't resist the dig.

"Nobody sent me. It was my idea."

I didn't want to get her mad again or lose points so I told her she was very attractive and how she turned me on. I went easy but she kept listening and I was getting signals. Damn! I'm no kid and her body was arching. I realized her blouse was unbuttoned more than before and her hand just lay there under my moving fingers without pulling away. Like our hands were going to have sex. I was getting so hard it hurt so I slid my hand off hers and under her skirt. She froze—didn't even quiver until I got my fingers right up there. So help me I know she liked it. I got my hand into her pants until I could feel the soft hair of her bush and the little tongue all soft and wet like gravy. I put my finger right up there and it went in so nice I could taste it. I lifted my left hand to touch her face and start mounting her and next thing I knew she grabbed my gun. Bitch! That woman was coming and she grabbed my gun!

She jumped up and held it over me. "Con!" she yelled. "Con!" He musta been watching he jumped up so fast.

If she'd kept her mouth shut it mighta been different. I coulda handled things. But she was fighting me and I had to protect myself. Everybody started to run over. I grabbed her legs. She fell on top of me and we wrestled for the gun. I pulled like crazy and it went off.

That's how it happened. I was so freaked out by then I didn't even hear the shot.

Con screamed a lot of shit at me. Duke was shouting and shoving them back with his rifle. Con moaned like a child. Flora didn't move the blood pouring out of her chest into the sand. Con pulled off his shirt and balled it up like a man plugging a hole in the dike. He couldn't stop the bleeding. I kept saying it was an accident. And then we knew she was dead. Holy shit.

The gun was on the ground somewhere. I couldna cared less. I just wanted to run out and throw up. It wasn't the blood—that didn't bother me. But feeling so totally screwed! Women have pulled things on me but that woman did a worldclass number. She musta been a poker nut! I'd never tell Duke the whole story. He'd bust his pants laughing.

Con got dumb. He musta seen the gun when he came over. Duke caught him reaching—the guy was on his knees with the dying broad—so he just kicked his arm a couple of stiff ones with his pointy-toed boot. Con howled. Everybody was howling by then about something. The music was still playing—sounded like "San Fernando Valley" would you believe? Unreal.

"Get her out of here!" Duke says. "Take her and clear out." That's what I mean about Duke being a swell guy. He coulda just blown Con's skull off right then and there. Everybody was carrying on. Abby and Mary went off howling like banshees Mary wanting to go with her sister and beating her breast about the deal blaming herself. Charles crying and telling everybody it was an accident. I think he was pissed about the trouble and Flora's crazy scheme she must have cooked up with Con. Maybe with Mary too so damn jittery about her baby dumpling. And Maybelle standing frozen not running to her mother but scared of Duke and scared of fallout and bombs and every friggin thing. A case that one. Not wrapped too tight.

Duke was fed up to his eyeballs. He'd really had it. He was going to clear them all out. I could feel it. I didn't know what I wanted but I was sick of the whole deal.

Maybe Charles triggered the rest of it offering to help Con take his dead wife out of the Cave. I think Grandpa wanted to get the thing over with so he could wash his hands of the mess. The two of them started carrying Flora out.

"Good riddance," said Duke.

Mary flipped. "They're coming back! My father and Con are coming back!" she's screaming at Duke.

"You telling me something?"

"They've got to come back!"

"Maybe you better go too. And Abby." Duke wasn't taking any more crap.

"All right!" she's shrieking. "We'll all go. Come here Maybelle. We're leaving." Yammering away while her father is helping the guy carry her sister's body out.

Charles is half out the door and if he didn't have his hands full he might have socked her it looked like. He's a survivor and he wants to get back in and he knows she doesn't have a clue when you got down to it. I guess we all were shook up. And she's getting into a hassle with her daughter.

Maybelle is telling her she doesn't want to go anyplace and Mary starts letting her have it. Then she starts on Duke again says he's to keep his hands off the kid and the kid wants her mother to shut the fuck up. Duke puts his hand on Maybelle's shoulder and Mary really starts having a baby.

"Get away from her!" she's yelling at Duke. "She's only a child. I can have you arrested! She's frail and you're taking advantage because she has a crippled leg!"

Well, then Maybelle starts having a baby. She went for her mother like a flying tackle. She grabbed Mary and was screaming in her face that she was no cripple and there wasn't anything wrong with her leg and the only thing wrong with her was her mother. What a couple of flakes! Hell I'd never have kids not even if they were bought and paid for and grown up already. Maybelle turned her back on her mother and went to Duke. You needed a scorecard at that point to figure out the teams.

The door closed kind of heavy. Charley leans against it like he was going to drop or else he was holding the door shut. We were two less now. Con sure wasn't going to make it back. In Duke's eyes he was through. Mine too.

Duke said we couldn't have any more trouble and he got everybody to agree. He also got them to agree he was boss. "For security reasons," he said. Pretty smooth.

Mary and Abby stood at the door with Charles. Then Grandma and Grandpa went off to sit on their side of the Cave. Mary sort of fidgets like she wants to leave but doesn't have the guts.

Finally she asks Duke if she can hand Con his things. "He doesn't even have a shirt on."

Duke lets her get some stuff together. I guess she put food in there too. She went out and sort of crept back in empty-handed looking dazed. She went off to sit with her head in her hands and Mommy and Daddykins clucking over her. I picked up my jean jacket and folded it into a flat pillow. Then I lay down and went to sleep.

eleven Maybelle

 I couldn't stop crying. Just the tears coming down. Was it for Aunt Flora? Roy being outside? Us being here? I sort of forgot about Jack and Julia. I was trying not to make noise or make a fuss. Didn't want to worsen things. I hated my mother and I didn't hate her. Or I was ashamed of hating her. If only things were simpler. Why oh why did she have to drag that up about my leg? Every day I tried to forget it, feel I wasn't different. Well I wasn't, hardly. I wore jeans and slacks that were tight around my butt but loose in the pant legs. You could only see the difference at the beach. Then I'd hear her tell somebody, "Maybelle's good-looking and you can hardly notice her leg." Oh, how that hurt.

She was stupid. I wondered why she stayed stupid even when I told here how I felt. So she knew what she was doing. Maybe she disliked me for some weird reason—did I remind her of Dad? He sure loved me. Whatever. It just came out cruel and I'd want to die but kill her first. Then I'd feel guilty, guilty, and remember it was hard bringing us up, even with the money from Grandpa. She liked Uncle Con a lot, everybody knew that. Aunt Flora did. Maybe Mom herself didn't know how much but that must have been hard too. I was really sick about Aunt Flora. The whole situation was totally freaky. Like there was a graveyard outside for her and we were sort of buried alive here in the Cave. I kept thinking we ought to have a funeral and flowers. For the whole mess of us! Crazy and sane ideas. I mean the same ideas were sane and crazy.

Mom should have gone out the door with Uncle Con. That's what she truly wanted. Looking for Roy? That's a hoot. Oh, sure she loves him, a thousand times more than me though she'll never admit it, but it's Con she was after. She would have stood bombs and dead bodies for that, ten Aunt Floras lying there stiff. And maybe that's what ached her the most, what freaked her out. As if her bad thoughts had killed her sister. She must have wanted her dead sometimes. I'm learning how mean people can be even if it's only their thoughts. That's the worst—hating someone and not being able to come out with it, keeping all the bad inside, feeling guilty, gnawing at yourself.

I learned another worst thing in the Cave with Aunt Flora: Her dying and my never having said anything especially nice to her. Not that I'd ever said anything unkind. Just sort of a blank. It was Uncle Con who came around, who wanted to take us places. My mother though, she must feel terrible. Like her secret dream coming true and it turns out to be a screaming nightmare. Imagine the kind of things my mother might have wanted to tell Aunt Flora—nice things—too late. She missed the last train.

Who wants to be outside anyway? Yes, as a home the Cave stinks. Damp, dark, it reminds me of a swamp. Count Dracula's basement. A funny odor. Like a funeral parlor before the flowers come. What a misery it'll be here—I want to go home! I wish Roy were around. He should have stayed with me. Jack and Julia can take care of themselves. Julia is two whole years older than me. Eighteen, same as Roy. Their parents leave her and Jack on their own with only the cleaning woman to supervise. What heaven! But you can have too much of a good thing. I like Jack and Julia even though they're spoiled, getting things they don't need and missing out on things they do. Some things anyway.

Julia's keen on going steady. Still she's going away to school, leaving Roy flat. She's not very sensitive. I miss Roy. Where is he? What is he doing? If only Mom could have grabbed him like she grabbed me. At least I have my Teddy bear, same one I've had since third grade. You need to have things to hold on to.

Mom is like the parents saying, "We love our children. Everything is for the children." Baloney. Why do they let wars happen? Like Roy says, "What about other people's children? Parents must love them too!" People just want to live. All those houses and families being blown up. Why am I supposed to hate people I don't even know? Uncle Con used to talk about war profits and oil and stuff. If there's war all the time, what'll be left to enjoy? Or anybody in one piece? Or healthy?

I thought of my room, its wallpaper with spring flowers, its white curtains and sunlight. I thought of *The Wizard of Oz*. "There's no place like home," said Dorothy, clicking the heels of her red shoes together, sending her home. I only had sandals.

We keep getting static on the radio—it could drive you crazy. Make you feel the world went away and left us.

I'm glad for Duke's CDs and all that sweet old music. He's nice to me. He doesn't treat me like a kid even though I keep holding a stuffed animal. He got a kick out of my little atomizer when I sprayed the air with cologne. I'm not afraid of him anymore. He knows how to take charge of things. Somebody has to.

We went and sat far back in the Cave down on the ledge where it was darkest and nobody could see us. He has a nice voice and he's been around the world. He told me about some of the places. His stories took me right out of the Cave. India! China! Imagine being where everybody looks so different and the food and climate are different. Even the time! He knows how to tell a story. We talked about what he did. I asked him and he told me. I was a little shocked at first thinking about the guns he'd sold and people getting killed with them. I remembered Uncle Con and the war profits but maybe it wasn't Duke's fault that he could sell things people wanted to buy. I don't feel bad about sitting with him because I don't think anybody really and truly is that upset about it. That's an awful thing to think but I see it that way. Grandpa Charles just wants things to settle down and Grandma Abby is chilling out. Mom and I aren't even speaking. It was like peace. A cease-fire. Burns tuned out and went to sleep. Sleep! Who could sleep?

Duke had his arm around me. He asked if he could move my Teddy bear beside him and I said yes. He came at me very slowly, very gently, like he was testing new territory every minute. He told me he admired me, the spunk I had speaking up to my mother. He said he thought I was beautiful. I mentioned my leg. He said he couldn't believe there was a thing wrong with me and he wanted to see the leg. I said it was so dark he couldn't see anything. So he pulled out the little light on his key chain. I took off my sandals.

He helped me take my jeans off. He had his rifle and guns on the other side of him. I felt his hands on my hips, like he was measuring. My bikini briefs didn't hide much.

He turned the little beam of light on my legs and said he couldn't see anything wrong and was I kidding him. I pointed to the right one—it looked more normal when I was lying down. Then he did something really sweet. He bent over and kissed that leg. He kissed it slowly as if he didn't want to stop as if it was important. Then he licked it and moved his hands up and down both my legs. I didn't know what to do what I was supposed to do. I'd been into making out with a couple of boys in high school because I was still proving I wasn't different from other girls. But I never had these feelings—so many and all mixed up. I was still a little scared of him from before but it got me more excited. He was licking the insides of my legs, moving up. I didn't want him to stop even though I was tense. He stopped and spread his jacket under me. He said he could get a blanket. I said no. I was just feeling no.

He had my briefs down—I could touch his hair—and he had his face right there. His breath was warm. The tip of his nose was massaging my clitoris and opening it up. I was rigid with fear and excitement, wanting him to do more, to taste me put his tongue there his finger anything. He said I was juicy and he suddenly swung upward and kissed me on the mouth his mouth still wet from me down there, so fresh I could taste myself.

He whispered in my ear, breathed into it, kept relaxing me bit by bit. I knew he was handling me carefully because he wanted something and wanted it the right way. We both knew he could have raped me, but he wasn't getting his kicks that way and I was grateful.

He put his arms around me like he was all the people in the world with all the love I wanted to be wrapped up in. It wasn't love—could it be?—but I felt good about myself. He pulled down his pants halfway. He kept his boots on.

He had me touch his penis. It was very hard and had a nice curve to it like my Mom's douche syringe. It felt big in the darkness and I didn't have much experience to compare it with. He started to enter me very slowly like I was something delicate he didn't want to break and that got me even more excited. I was so wet I thought I was peeing.

He seemed very happy from what he was whispering. He took a long time. He'd rest and start up again making it last. Then he sort of groaned and shuddered. When he stopped he reached down into his pants pocket and got a large handkerchief. I thought I needed a bath towel.

"Was it OK?" he asked me. "Was it good?"

"Yes," I answered. I wasn't lying.

twelve   Armageddon

From a distance they could have been ants, buffed by a hard moon that followed their path. Closer they might have been deer, tracking through dead leaves, low bushes, and spindly oaks. Up close: Martha and John, accompanied by Trudy; Jack, assisted by Julia and Roy; Jeremiah, at a reluctant pace, followed by Joe, who now carried a rifle. His overalls bulged at the left pocket. A few feet behind: Mike, Bob, and Tim. They, too, carried rifles.

Ahead, at the foot of the incline, the Cave doors, framed in rock, stood impassively closed. In the clearing a man was kneeling, as if in prayer, over a still figure stretched out at the edge of the rise, some twenty feet from the Cave entrance. As the group neared, Roy pushed his way forward and ran.

"Uncle Con!"

In the moonlight, naked to the waist, Con's anguished figure resembled that of some primitive man keening over his fallen mate. Although he uttered no sound, with arms outstretched he swayed over the body of his wife as if invoking heavenly aid that was not forthcoming. A suitcase and a shopping bag set beside him suggested that he had returned from or was about to embark on a strange unaccountable journey.

Con looked up at Roy and opened his mouth. He made a funny gurgling sound and turned his gaze back to the woman's face. From the neck down she was covered with a sheet that Roy recognized as a tablecloth. The woman's face looked thin and shadowed. Aunt Flora.

"Oh, Uncle Con! Is she—what happened?" He threw his arms around the man and knelt beside him. The group gathered in curiosity.

"She's dead," Con said hoarsely. "Shot. In the Cave."

"Who did it?"

"Burns. He's in there. They're all in there."

"Maybe that's the man who killed the guard!" Martha blurted.

"Killed?" Trudy shrieked. "Now you're saying *killed*? Show us where they took him. Show us!" She held out a gun shakily.

"Put that down!" shouted Martha. "We didn't do anything!"

"Maybe you *should* have done something!"

"Show us!" said Joe, advancing toward Martha and John. "Boys," he told his brothers, "keep watch here." He gave his flashlight to Martha. "Show us," he repeated. The four disappeared behind the Cave entrance.

A little apart from the rest, Jack sat on a rock with Julia beside him. He was touching his swollen ankle. Con's lament poured into the silence. Though they only knew him slightly, his awesome grief had struck them dumb.

Jeremiah offered to say a prayer. Con turned on him with a fierce "No, thanks," and lapsed back into silence. The preacher wrung his hands. "That murderer must be in there!"

"Don't worry," said Mike. "We'll smoke him out if he is."

Roy got up. He stood uncertainly by the Cave door. "Get back, kid," said Mike.

"My family's in there," Roy insisted. "My mother and sister and grand-parents."

"What the bejesus they doing in there? What the hell they doing with a murderer?"

Roy was afraid to answer. How could he explain Con and Flora outside, Flora dead, killer inside with Roy's family? How to explain his own exclusion?

The investigators were returning. In their slow procession, Martha had her arm around Trudy, who was wailing. Joe and John were carrying a man's body.

The two men set down their burden. Trudy collapsed beside it but Joe pulled her up. "No time for that, girl," he said, not unkindly. "We got something to do here, first. We're gonna get that rat out of his hole. What'd you say his name was?" He turned to Con.

Con remained silent.

"What's his name?" shouted Joe.

"Burns. There are two of them. Duke and Burns," he quickly added.

"OK," Joe announced. "Get back folks. Gonna be fireworks here."

"What are you going to do?" asked Roy.

"You'll see. Get back."

"I told you my family's in there!" cried Roy. "My family! They were just looking for shelter—"

"So they joined a coupla murderers killed my brother and your aunt! What a buncha lowlifes! Get back or somebody's going to get wasted right here and now." He turned to the Cave door. "Burns! Duke! Come on out, you bastards, or we'll blow you to hell!" He was holding an oval object in his left hand.

"What's that?" Roy was terrified.

"Ever see a grenade? It's a war souvenir I been keeping. I'm sentimental."

"You can't use that!"

"Get the hell back, kid!"

"There are innocent people in there! You could bury them all!"

"Nobody's innocent. Get back."

Jeremiah rushed over. "It's a shelter for everyone! We can all use it—like David in the Cave of Adullam! Blast the door and you'll bring down the whole place. Warn them, for the love of God. Give them a chance to come out. They're human beings!"

"You hot to save your own skin, Preach? OK. One more time: Everybody get back! Me and my brothers are handling this show."

They stepped back and withdrew to opposite sides: Trudy to the right, near her husband's body, a few feet from Jack and Julia; the others to the left of the rise. Con, dazed, stood up. "You can't—you can't—!" he was crying.

"Get away, you asshole!" screamed Joe. Con didn't move. "Burns! Duke!" Joe shouted. "We know you're there. Come out or we'll bomb you out!"

Mike, Bob, and Tim knelt and aimed their rifles. Roy dashed to the Cave door. "Momma! Momma!" he yelled and banged at the metal. "Maybelle! It's Roy! Please come out! Get away from the door! Momma! He's got a grenade!"

"Wait!" shouted Con in horror as he saw Joe pull the pin.

"Get away you dumb idiot!" Joe shouted to Roy. "It's coming!"

Roy turned and saw the grenade whiz past his head. He merged with the boom and crash and rumbling as the door and the mantle of rocks hurtled down into screaming flesh and the eruption of chaos inside, bonding with death on the West Coast traveling eastward and everywhere everywhere ending—did he witness a deer leaping away?—with nothing more to figure out.

Like an earthquake, the ponderous roof of the Cave imploded tremors into the ground, sent waves of noise and dust toward the onlookers until the crashing and crumbling subsided. An occasional rock tumbled toward the cairn piled at the entrance. And then the movement stopped, its thunder rolling out to meet the silence. A trembly silence. Shock.

Jack, Julia, and Con rushed to Roy, who lay prone with his left arm buried in rubble. The three frantically pulled away the stones, freeing his arm. Con turned him over and saw that his face was a bloody mask. He was dead.

Julia started moaning and sobbing. Jack picked up a rock and, hobbling toward Joe, hurled it with hysterical rage. He missed.

"Try that again, sonny, and I'll blast your guts!" warned Joe.

Julia rose. "Stop it! Stop it!" she yelled, tugging Jack's arm. He shook her off and picked up another rock. Joe fired, nicking his left arm.

"Next time I'll aim different!"

"Murderer!" Julia shrieked as her brother fell, groaning. Con picked up a rock and ran to Joe who hit him with his rifle butt.

"Let's get away!" Martha called to Jeremiah and John.

"C'mon, Jer!" urged John as he and Martha started up the rise.

"Where the hell you going?" shouted Bob to the retreating pair. He fired over their heads and they flattened themselves against the ground.

"Come back here! Nobody moves till I say so!" Joe ordered.

But Jeremiah was running toward Con and Joe, brandishing his Bible. Joe was about to hit Con again in the face. "Stop! Stop! In the name of the Lord!" Jeremiah commanded.

"Beat it Preacher, it's not your business!" snarled Joe.

"In the name of Jesus!" said Jeremiah, waving his Bible.

"What the devil you know about Jesus, you two-bit hustler?" asked Joe.

Con suddenly reached over and pulled Joe's ankles, knocking him to the ground. The rifle fell to one side and the two men wrestled. Bob rushed over, aiming at Con who rolled back and forth with Joe in the struggle.

"No!" shouted Jeremiah. "Enough! Enough!" The Bible fell from his hand as he stooped to pick up a rock. Bob fired twice. Con moaned, then lay quiet. Joe stood up. Jeremiah held out the rock.

No one spoke. Even the crickets and katydids were silent. As she cradled her brother in her arms, Julia looked back at Roy. Her steady weeping cast filaments of sound over the silent landscape, the world outside the Cave and the wreck within it, all the fragmented Earth that lay beneath the hard moon.

"Let's clear out," Joe snapped at his brothers. He turned to Jeremiah who stood immobilized, still clutching the rock. "You want to say something, Preach? You got something to tell the brethren here? About the Lord's vengeance? You gonna tell us some shit and you standing there ready to knock heads with the rest of us? What you got in your hand, preacherman? Drop it! Drop it, you sonofabitch faker!"

Jeremiah let the rock fall. He thought wildly: On this rock I build my Church.

"You've killed him! My God you've killed him!" Jeremiah shouted.

"He ain't dead," said Joe, in disgust. "Come on guys. Let's get Harry." The four brothers descended a ways toward Trudy, who kept vigil over her husband's body. The men picked up their brother's corpse and retreated up the hill, Trudy following. They disappeared among the trees.

Jeremiah surveyed the ghostly battlefield: Julia whimpering, fussing over Jack. Con bleeding. He went to Con.

A bullet had struck the man's right shoulder and his eyes were closed. Jeremiah took out the clean white handkerchief that Martha always placed in his pocket. He tried to staunch the wound.

Martha and John approached. "We may be getting killed out here," said the woman. "We ought to get back to the van."

Jeremiah turned angrily. "What you talking about, sister? There's people need help around here. You gone blind? Go help with that kid down there," he indicated Jack. "Do something! John, give me a hand with this one."

Was God saying something to him at last? That cold, vengeful, self-righteous Deity—where was the Mercy? Weren't people punishing each other without the help of a Holy Wrecker from outside? Wasn't there enough pain here for the whole Universe? God had been quiet with him for so long. He seemed to be looking the other way, ignoring salvation and anything else Jeremiah was trying to preach. Could it be that he was getting the message wrong? Maybe that wasn't what the world needed, another burden of empty rules and promises—what had the man called him—"a hustler"? Long ago as a boy he had been right when he felt the simple urge to help people. And now here he was, ministering to bodies, confronting the plain limits of human flesh, of hearts that knew only to keep on beating.

He glanced at the moon. Was God there in that faintly smiling face, that moon face looking down with equanimity on love and death and torture as if nothing mattered at all to it, as if earthly concerns were a macabre joke? Was God in the silent Cave of death, the tomb from which the stones would not be rolled away?

It no longer seemed important that Jeremiah's work be ritualized, that his acts be sorted into handy categories. The grenade had shaken the ground beneath him. Everything was shifting and had altered, and he was trying to read the meaning.

He knew there was no hope of anyone left alive in the Cave but he called to them anyway until he was hoarse. He walked to the rubble, that tomb, that wound of humanity and kept calling and listening in vain. Then he lifted his arms in prayer. "Bless these people, O Lord," he cried. "Forgive them. Take them to Thy bosom."

He closed his eyes, wishing he were a boy suspended in grace at the banister of the orphanage staircase, stars bursting from his head and a host of angels like a nimbus of clouds and God with his golden robes taking him to sit on his knee and the singing, the singing! I am Thy servant, Lord.

And the nuns standing around and the children like a hushed choir wait-ing: Tell us (was that Martha?), what do you see? And his eyes rolling up-ward in bliss. And then the threadbare years of preaching Christ crucified out of a dingy van, preaching Salvation and the Day of Judgment, at first of-fering them uncontaminated by dirt roads—what was uncontaminated now?—and eventually trivializing them, yes, trivializing them into shibbo-leths, turning them into celestial coat hooks for garments nobody wore. Now there were suffering bodies around him, bodies he could see and touch. Might it not all be simple, coming down to this: one person clean-ing the wounds of another? And beyond the moment, the mercy of for-giveness, of not inflicting any wounds at all.

From an anguish of unknowing deep in his soul issued the silent cry: A sign, Lord! But there was only Con's groan as John staunched his wound with Jeremiah's handkerchief and Jack getting his arm bandaged.

"We got to get these people to the van," he told John.

"Sure, Jer. We'll do it." As the two men prepared to lift Con, Jeremiah felt a soft object underfoot: his Bible. He stooped to pick it up. Dusting it off carefully with his fingers, he slipped it back into his pocket.